I0640178

PRAISE FOR ALEX MASON

"It is brutal, wastes no time, and is full of action."

AMAZON REVIEW

"Better than Bond, Bourne, or Reacher."

AMAZON REVIEW

"For fans of Clancy, Mitch App, and Brad Taylor."

AMAZON REVIEW

"Same level as Patterson or Baldacci."

AMAZON REVIEW

"This book is filled with action, intrigue, espionage, and everything else lovers of a good thriller want."

AMAZON REVIEW

ALL THE KING'S MEN

AN ALEX MASON THRILLER

DAVID ARCHER

BLAKE BANNER

RIGHTHOUSE

Copyright © 2024 by Right House

All rights reserved.

The characters and events portrayed in this ebook are fictitious. Any similarity to real persons, living or dead, is coincidental and not intended by the author.

No part of this book may be reproduced in any form or by any electronic or mechanical means, including information storage and retrieval systems, without written permission from the author, except for the use of brief quotations in a book review.

ISBN-13: 978-1-63696-309-9

ISBN-10: 1-63696-309-9

Cover design by: Damonza

Printed in the United States of America

www.righthouse.com

www.instagram.com/righthousebooks

www.facebook.com/righthousebooks

twitter.com/righthousebooks

ALEX MASON THRILLERS
Odin (Book 1)
Ice Cold Spy (Book 2)
Mason's Law (Book 3)
Assets and Liabilities (Book 4)
Russian Roulette (Book 5)
Executive Order (Book 6)
Dead Man Talking (Book 7)
All The King's Men (Book 8)
Flashpoint (Book 9)
Brotherhood of the Goat (Book 10)
Dead Hot (Book 11)
Blood on Megiddo (Book 12)
Son of Hell (Book 13)

PROLOGUE

COLONEL IAN CAMERON, RETIRED, LATE OF THE Central Intelligence Agency, looked out at his audience and smiled with the confidence of a man who has faced violent death so many times he has forgotten how to be scared.

"This book," he said, "is the story of my life," he paused a moment to give a brief, ironic laugh, "or at least that part of it, after I was eighteen, when the illegal things I did had the blessing of the Federal Government." There was laughter around the brightly lit room. "That made life a lot easier, I can tell you. Those first eighteen years will have to remain my secret. Let me just say that the midwife's first word when I was born was 'Oops!' and my mother's first six words to the midwife were, 'What is the policy on returns?'"

There was more laughter, almost an uproar. They'd had enough wine and brandy to laugh at anything, and the colonel's delivery was good.

"I know," he went on. "I could have been a stand-up comedian, but the comedians make this stuff up." He paused and became serious. "But what I'm doing is telling you the truth." The laughter died away. "When I was eighteen I joined Delta Force, which you are told doesn't actually exist. I can tell you it does. It is very real. When I joined them I had the moral and ethical standards of a Mexican second-hand car dealer." He smiled and shook his head. "I'll tell you! I once had a meeting with Bill Clinton, you can read all about it in the book, and he left the meeting in tears, sobbing, 'Lord forgive me, I have seen the error of my ways!' Seriously, he went and joined the Quakers after that. I met Hillary and she kept calling me Lord."

They were in stitches again, and one guy was slapping his thigh.

"I'm kidding, that never happened. Not like that, anyway. But from Delta I was recruited into the Central Intelligence Agency. They told me they'd recruited me because, in the psych evaluation I had scored zero in moral inhibitions. They said there was no moral—or immoral—place I was not prepared to go. And I gotta tell you, back then, that was true. There are people like that. I have met them. The Mexican cartels are made up of people like that. But what is worrying, my friends, is when Western security agencies, those agencies charged with protecting democracy and our Federal Government, recruit you *because* you are like that. I should have been in a mental institution, or better still on Death Row. But they couldn't do that to me because in the beginning I was too valuable to them, and later because everything I had done I had done with their blessing. And besides."

He looked around the room at the faces, wide-eyed and wondering, warm with admiration.

"Don't ask me how it happened. I don't really know myself. But you look into enough pleading eyes, you see enough orphaned children, enough destroyed families, and something begins to happen inside of you. I am not just talking about the *hundreds of thousands* of people murdered and orphaned in Mexico, so that those bastards can become billionaires. I am talking also about driving through DC, Philly or Chicago, or any other city in the USA, and seeing the junkies, the junkies' children, the wasted lives, the hollow, uncomprehending eyes too wasted even to plead. I am talking about seeing that and knowing that you enabled it. That you made it possible."

He paused a long time, leaning on the lectern and staring at the floor.

"Something," he said and looked out at his audience again, "something inside you begins to stir and wake up, and you know that somehow it is wrong, and you have to stop. I don't know if there's a god, and if there is I don't know if it is a monster or a god of love and forgiveness. And I have no idea how to define good and evil. But what I can tell you is that I know in my bones that what I did for all those years was wrong, and now, somehow, I have to atone. So fifty percent of the proceeds of this book will go to setting up a foundation to help children who are the victims of parents who abuse or trade in drugs." There was applause. When it died down he added, jabbing his finger toward the cardboard display by the door, "But equally important is that, if I must atone, the bastards who recruited me, who shielded me and enabled me to do the things I did, must atone also. There are pillars of society in this country who have grown rich—fabulously rich—on the pain and suffering of millions of men, women and children from Chiapas and Yucatan to Chihuahua and Sonora. This book will be published in a month. Advanced sales are already through the roof. Good! Because when this book hits the stands, my friends, heads are going to roll from the White House to the National Palace in Mexico City! The time has come for a lot of people to take responsibility for what they have done. I am the first, but believe me, I am not the last!"

The room erupted in applause. People got to their feet, clapping, whistling and shouting. From a table just in front of the lectern, Araminta Whitley, his publisher, stood and came to join him. They hugged, taking care to keep looking out at the audience, where cameras were flashing, and after a moment she approached the lectern and the microphone.

"Dear friends...dear friends..." The applause and the noise gradually died down and people returned to their seats. "Dear friends," she said again, "we are today in the presence of a truly remarkable man who, raised in an environment of violence, crime and cruelty, set out to take control—to own his own life. And though he had to go through hell to get there, he eventually found his own humanity and is now ready and willing—having faced his own monsters—to face the monsters in Washington DC and elsewhere, and bring them to account. This book, when it hits the stands in one month, will send seismic shock waves through the Capitol and the White House *and* the Pentagon. Make a note of the title and if you haven't done so already, order your copy now! *Sex Drugs and Rock 'n' Roll at the White House!*"

They hugged again, this time more intimately, among the sudden noise of people breaking into conversation, rising from their tables or calling for drinks. As he released her he said, "In my day they'd have put out a hit on me. These days I don't think they'd dare."

She laughed. "I hope you're right. I want at least another two books out of you. And I *want* that autobiography!"

He grinned. "I plead the fifth. I'll call you tomorrow. Maybe we can have lunch."

She wagged a finger at him. "If I haven't heard from you by eleven, I'll call you!"

He held both her hands and squeezed them, then turned and moved through the crowd, stopping here and there to exchange a few words, kiss the ladies and slap the men's shoulders.

Finally he made it to the hotel lobby, where he paused to pull a pack of Camels from his tuxedo pocket and poke one in his mouth. He flipped open an old, battered Zippo, leaned into the flame and headed toward the door. On his way he grinned at the worried-looking concierge. "Lifetime of breaking rules, I'm not going to stop now, right? Don't worry, I'm on my way out."

Outside, at the bottom of the red-carpeted steps he paused beside the grotesque gilt lamp, thrust his right hand in his trouser pocket and took a drag. He inhaled the smoke deep into his lungs, then raised his chin to blow a long stream of smoke into the night air.

Across the road an old guy with a long beard and a hat was leaning against the wall, watching him. The trees of Central Park towered above him, and beside him he had a small dog in an ancient pram. Colonel Ian Cameron touched his forehead with two fingers in a salute. Choices, he told himself, it's all about the choices you make.

He turned right, and though it was cold, he strolled. He

liked New York. He liked New York at night. He liked the lights and the people and the skyscrapers that had once been futuristic and were now classical and reminiscent of Orson Welles and Scott Fitzgerald. He passed the Pulitzer Fountain, not sure where he was going, but thinking about where to stop for a nightcap.

That was when he saw the gorgeous brunette walking toward him in a hurry and smiling. She was ten feet away in a scarlet dress that was hugging her like it never wanted to let go, and a cute red pillbox on her head, when she said, "Colonel? Colonel Ian Cameron? Don't you remember me?"

He took a drag as she drew closer and said, "I feel like I ought to."

She giggled and placed a red satin-gloved hand on his chest. "There is a man behind you with a Maxim 9 pointed at your lower back. It will cripple you for life, but we'll get you to a doctor in that SUV," she pointed to a black Mercedes that had pulled up by the sidewalk with its hazards flashing, "before you die. And you'll live the rest of your life as a pathetic cripple."

She came in close and took hold of his satin lapels. "So why don't you do the smart thing and get in the back of the car, so we can talk in private?"

Two guys in suits had climbed out of the SUV and had approached them where they stood. He turned and saw she hadn't lied about the guy behind him. He figured they hadn't killed him—and he knew they could have—so they wanted something. That meant it was safer to go along than to try and fight or run. He shrugged.

"If I come along quietly, can I take you to dinner later?"

"Oh," she gave a laugh that was as funny as swimming naked in a frozen lake in Siberia, "you *really* don't want to do that."

They bundled him discretely into the Merc. A few people glanced, but he wasn't struggling and the people around him were smiling and chatting. So nobody raised the alarm. Then they were sliding the doors closed and two guys climbed in the cab, and the SUV pulled out into the traffic, nice and steady.

In the back the colonel looked at the two guys next to him, and the beautiful woman opposite. Something in her eyes made him uneasy.

"Where are we going?"

It was violent and unexpected. The guy on his right grabbed his wrist and twisted savagely while the guy on his left grabbed his head and forced him forward, so his brow was pressed on his knees. The woman pulled up his jacket and wrenched his shirt out of his pants. Then he felt a piercing, burning agony in his back.

They let him go and he sat upright, gasping. Hot rage was burning in his head, but the cannons of two Maxim 9s stopped him before he could act. The woman said, "Easy, Colonel. See this?" She showed him her cell phone. "Yes, it's my phone, but it is also a detonator. I have just injected a capsule of high explosive next to your spine. It's not enough to bring down a plane or demolish a building, but it's enough to blow your spine in half. All I have to do is dial the right number. So from this moment on, you are going to do just exactly as I say. Do you *comprende, compadre*?"

"You bitch. Where are you taking me?"

"Oh, don't worry, you'll like it," she said. "You and me

are going to Mexico. We're going to visit some old friends of yours. They will be really happy to see you again, now that you've become a famous author, an' all.'"

Colonel Ian Cameron sank back into the black leather seat. He had taken care not to offend or upset Ismael Zamora or Francisco Gallardo. He had spoken to them and cleared everything with them first. The rest of them at the Company, the White House and the Capitol he didn't give a damn about. But Sinaloa were his friends, his tribe. He did not want to upset them. He eyed the beautiful killer opposite him and wondered if they had sent her. If they had, by the look in her eyes, he had offended them.

And badly.

ONE

At three minutes past eleven the next morning, Araminta Whitley stood at the sixteenth-floor window of her office at Oddhouse Publishing, on the corner of 55th and Broadway, tapping her foot. She sighed deeply and picked up her phone. "Jamilla, get me Colonel Cameron on the phone, please."

"Will do."

She hung up and stood scanning the taxis far below. When her phone rang two minutes later she forced herself to count to four before answering.

"Yes?"

She was surprised not to hear Jamilla's voice. It was a man's, vaguely familiar.

"Araminta?"

"Yes...?"

"This is Alasdair Cameron, Ian's brother."

"Oh!" She laughed, like it was funny it should be him

and not somebody else. "I didn't recognize you. How *are* you?"

He sounded like he'd been asleep for the past fifty years and wasn't sure he wanted to wake up.

"Well, I'm a little worried, Araminta. You see, Ian said he was going to see you last night, for his book launch—"

"That's not a reason to be worried, darling."

"Um," he wasn't sure if he was supposed to laugh or not, so he did something odd with his voice, like a small cough, and went on, "that's why I'm calling you. You see, he didn't come home last night. And since he's been back to New York, he has been very particular about either coming home, or telling me where he is going to be. A security thing, or something. And you know yourself, he is very punctual, always."

She was quiet for a moment. "He lives with you?"

"We share the old family home on East 78th Street, just by the park," he added inconsequentially. "He said he'd be home around midnight, but there's no sign of him, and I can't get an answer from his phone. Do you know where he is?"

She could feel a hot bead of anxiety in her belly, but she laughed. "You know what an old scoundrel he is! He left the launch around eleven and probably went to a bar and got drunk with some gorgeous babe. I am expecting him now. We are supposed to have a meeting before lunch. I'll tell him off for you and get him to call as soon as he comes in."

"Thank you, Araminta. I *am* worried. I..." He hesitated, then gave a sigh that was very sad. "I really think he has gone too far this time."

He didn't wait for a reply. He just hung up and left her

with her phone pressed to her ear, looking at the yellow cabs far below. They were collecting and delivering their passengers, but not one of them had Colonel Ian Cameron onboard.

She stepped out of her office and looked down at her secretary, who had a telephone to her ear. Jamilla looked up at her boss and shook her head.

"Nothing. It just says his cell is switched off."

"Keep trying, honey."

"Will do, Boss."

At twelve noon Oddhouse himself phoned from the top floor.

"Mini, darling, how goes it with your barbarian from the CIA? We want him working on part two yesterday at the latest."

"Rupe, he was supposed to be here at eleven. I've had Jamilla calling his cell every ten minutes for the last hour, and to make it worse his brother phoned saying he didn't go home last night."

"Shit!" And then, "This is either a blessing or a damned disaster. Have you called the cops?"

"No..."

"Well call them, for goodness's sake! If somebody has killed him..." There was a thrill in his voice. "Do you know what that would do for sales? We get a ghost to write his unfinished autobiography—no pun intended—*To Live by the Sword*! No, no—*To Live and Die by the Sword*!"

"Rupert, you can't sack me, can you?"

"Not really, why?"

"Then go screw yourself!"

"Call the cops!"

"No, I'm going to call someone else. Leave it to me."

She hung up and called a Washington DC number. It rang once and an efficient, female voice answered, "This is the office of Senator Walther Gannett, how may I help you?"

"Tell Walther it's Araminta and I need to talk to him right now. It's urgent!"

"Hold the line please, Ms Whitley." There was a moment's silence and then the well-groomed voice of Senator Walther Gannett came on the line.

"Mini, sweetheart, have you finally decided to publish my autobiography?"

"I'm waiting till you become president or, better still, notorious. Walt. Listen, are you still involved in national security committees and all that crap you dabble in?"

"That's why you sleep secure in your bed at night, baby."

"Sure, it has nothing to do with my two Rottweilers. Who was that guy you told me about at George's dinner party at The Chapel? You said he was a genius and ran some kind of outfit that was above top secret and you couldn't tell me about it, only you were trying to get me to hit the sack with you...? You remember?"

"Oh, yeah. I shouldn't have done that. You should try to forget, Mini. They just call him Nero. Apparently he once burned down a restaurant or a hotel or something because the chef made him mad. The caviar was not beluga or it was two degrees too cold or something. But he won't write an autobiography for you."

"That's not what I want. I need to talk to him."

"You can't just talk to Nero, honey. I'm not sure he really even exists."

"You talk to him."

"Well, yeah, I know how to…"

"Listen, tell him Colonel Ian Cameron has disappeared. If you get me an interview with him, I'll get you a ghost-writer and we'll publish your autobiography."

"You serious? I mean, are you serious that Cameron has disappeared?"

"I am serious."

"Are you going ahead with publication?"

"Of course!"

"Of course, right. OK, I'll talk to someone. I'll do my best, but I can't guarantee anything. Like I said, he doesn't really exist."

She hung up and immediately called Jamilla.

"Still nothing, Boss."

"OK, leave it, start calling around all the hospitals."

She didn't wait for a reply. She hung up, went to her desk and tried to keep busy. She kept telling herself Cameron was a rogue and he'd probably got drunk and gone back with some dame to her place and he would call in the next few minutes, or an hour. But she knew from the hollow feeling she had in her gut that she was kidding herself. That just wasn't Ian's style. Underneath his devil-may-care exterior, he was serious, punctual and efficient.

At one PM Jamilla came in to say there was no record of a Colonel James Cameron having been admitted to a hospital in New York last night or this morning.

At two o'clock her telephone rang. The screen told her the number was not known. She tried to remain cool and answered, "This is Araminta Whitely,"

"Miss Whitley, you asked your friend, Senator Walther Gannett to pull strings and arrange for me to call you."

"Oh, are you..."

"I am. I must tell you that it is unheard of for me to make such a call and I have severely reprimanded the senator. This telephone call is not happening and will not show on any records. Are we clear?"

"Oh, yes, I am sorry..."

"There is no need for you to apologize. You did not compel me to telephone, I undertook to do so of my own free will. You are publishing a book by Colonel Ian Cameron."

"That's correct. Yes, I am."

"*Sex, Drugs and Rock 'n' Roll at the White House.*"

"That's the one."

"A suitably sordid, vulgar title for a sordid, vulgar work. It names names, as the saying goes. And he has now disappeared."

She filled him in as to the details, then added, "Walther said you were a genius and a rare man of honor in a world of rats."

"Indeed?"

"I mean, if he had been assassinated, it would do wonders for sales, but I like Ian, and I'd hate for anything to happen to him."

"Quite. It is usually preferable to avoid assassination. Not always, but usually. In this case it would tend to confirm his allegations and would thus be avoided. I will send somebody to talk to you. They'll be in touch. Good day, Miss Whitley."

He had hung up before she could answer and she was left with the peculiar sensation of not being sure if the phone call had happened at all.

AT ODIN HEADQUARTERS on Wilson Avenue, in Arlington, Nero pressed a button and disconnected the call to Oddhouse Publishing. He pursed his lips a moment and raised his eyes to look at me. "Why," he asked, "do people who shouldn't keep writing memoirs they oughtn't? It is an epidemic."

I said, "Am I going to New York?"

"I don't know. Colonel Ian Cameron is not a lovable scoundrel, Alex. He is a monster. It is possible..." He trailed off and dialed a number. It rang a couple of times and one of those English, clipped, stiff-upper-lip voices answered.

"Nero, what can I do for you?"

"Brigadier, you are familiar with the name Colonel Ian Cameron."

"I am."

"Is he on one of your lists?"

"If he's not he should be, but we are curious about this book he's about to publish. Why do you ask?"

"Somebody may have beaten you to the punch. Last night he disappeared. It was not one of your operatives?"

"No. With a bit of luck he'll have drunk himself to death in some dive in a backstreet somewhere."

Nero thrust out his lower lip. "Perhaps, but it seems to me there may be people who want him dispatched at the moment, or at least punished, *pour encourager les autres*. Some of them could be people of interest to us."

"Well, good luck. If you need anything, give us a shout."

He disconnected the call. "Alex,"

"Yes, sir."

"Go to New York, speak to Miss Araminta Whitley, find out what has happened to the colonel, who has done it and for what reason. This may afford us an opportunity to rip up a few ugly weeds from our garden. Allegations in books can be refuted and denied, but if somebody has panicked and resorted to murder, then perhaps we can catch them *sanguis in manibus!*"

I stood. "You know me, there is nothing I like better than a bit of *sanguis in manibus*. I'll call you when I get there."

"There is no need for that." He reached for a file, opened it and started reading. "Call me when you have something."

"As long as you're OK." I opened the door. "I wouldn't want you worrying about me or anything."

"That will be fine," he said, and dismissed me with his fingertips.

I paused in Lovelock's office, ostensibly to ask her about booking me a flight to New York. Lovelock is five-foot eleven in her bare feet, her skin is purple-black, her eyes are enormous and almond-shaped, and she has the kind of curves that cause men to walk into lampposts. Not only that, she moves with the grace of a panther and her voice is like hot chocolate laced with an especially fine whiskey.

"You want to book me a flight to New York, Lovelock?"

"When for?" She asked it like it was really immoral and she enjoyed it.

"I have to be there today. You want to come with me? I know a place we could dine…"

She leaned forward with her chin on her hands and her fingers framing her perfect face. She smiled. "Oh, Alex, I would *love* that. I'll get my husband to pick us up in half an hour."

"You're cruel, Lovelock. Cruel."

"Poor Alex. But you know what? By the time I book it, you get to the airport, check in...you may as well drive. Four hours. The way you drive, maybe three and a half." I made for the door. She called, "I'll book you in at the Plaza. They have *really* comfy beds."

Lovelock wasn't wrong. It was a chance to put my new Factory Five, 450 bhp Shelby Cobra through its paces, and I made it in three hours and forty-five minutes; and by the time I got there I wanted to do it all over again. Instead I headed for the south end of the park, four blocks past Columbus Circle on Broadway, and managed to squeeze into a space outside Citibank.

Through the revolving glass and steel doors in Oddhouse Plaza, I crossed the gleaming marble lobby and let one of the five elevators take me to the sixteenth floor. When I stepped out of the sliding doors I was in another lobby. This one looked like it was made of polished toffee. Even the reception desk was made of amber marble, with a logo of an open book with a pop-up crooked house emerging from it. I figured it was a hangover from the early days when the company published only children's books. Today it was one of the biggest corporations on the planet.

The girl behind the desk had a frilly lace blouse, a string of pearls around her neck, a dark bun behind her neck and pretty dark eyes. I told her, "I'm here to see Araminta Whitley. She's expecting me but she doesn't know my name."

She smiled and squinted and cocked her head on one side. I said, "Tell her it's Alex Mason, from DC."

"Comics?"

"The city where the president lives. Washington."

"Oh," she buzzed and singsonged, "Ms. Whitley, I have a Mr. Alex Mason here for you from Washington DC." She pressed a button and smiled at me. "You were right. She was expecting you, and she didn't know your name."

She told me where the door was and a moment later I knocked and entered. It was a large, corner office. The walls were lined with bookcases and where there were no books, the walls held framed book covers. Her desk was littered with manuscripts and she, a handsome woman in her mid-forties, was striding across the floor to meet me with both hands reaching for mine.

"Mr. Mason? Alex? May I call you Alex? I'm Araminta." She grasped my hand and didn't so much shake it as squeeze it. "This has been one of the—no, scrub that, it *has* been *the* longest day of my *life!* Thank you so much for coming. Will you sit?"

She took rapid steps to adjust a chair at her desk. Then stopped and turned.

"You are... You said Washington, I mean..."

I smiled. "Nero sent me to talk to you about Colonel Ian Cameron. I am the man you were expecting."

She sighed and sagged, like the repressed sigh was the only thing keeping her upright. "Thank God."

I sat in the chair and frowned at her.

"We are going to need to go over this in baby steps, Araminta. I need to know what made you call Nero," I smiled and raised my eyebrows, "and how you knew *how* to call Nero, why you thought this would be of interest to him, and, when we've gone through that, I need you to tell me in minute detail exactly what happened."

She leaned her ass against the desk and crossed her arms. She eyed me a moment, then started to speak.

"You probably don't know this. Most people don't. But, publishing houses, especially big corporate publishing houses like Oddhouse, wield a lot more power than you might expect. We pull a lot of strings behind the scenes. You'd be amazed at how seriously the 'powers that be,'" she made little quote signs with her fingers, "take the whole issue of what books get published and become major bestsellers each year—and which ones don't. I was told not so long ago by a recent president that Hollywood and the major publishing houses are the most powerful tools in social engineering that Western Powers have at their disposal, more so even than Twitter, whatever Elon may think."

"I can believe that."

"So major editors like me, in major publishing houses like this, get invited to events, parties and dinners where they rub shoulders with very powerful people who sometimes get drunk. I was at a party a while back at a Texas ranch which shall remain nameless, and Senator Walther Gannett was there. He got drunk and started talking about a man he had met during a briefing to a Senate Committee on national security. The man was vast, rude, terrifyingly intelligent and insufferably arrogant and blunt. His name was Nero—nothing else—and nobody at the briefing knew what department he was attached to, but they all knew he was probably the most powerful, dangerous man in the room."

I made a mental note to have Senator Gannett

kneecapped in the near future and started to ask, "So what made you…"

"Quite aside from the fact that he sounded fascinating, if you knew how much is riding on this novel, if you knew the shock waves that will rock through DC when this hits the newsstands, you would realize that, the moment I understood that something had happened to Ian, I *knew* that I needed somebody very special to look for him and help him."

"So you called your friend Senator Gannett."

"Exactly."

"Ms. Whitley, Araminta, Nero is a sort of code name for the man who is the head of the Office of the Director of Intelligence Networks. He deals with threats from Russia, China, North Korea, Middle Eastern conflicts…" I smiled. "You can't call him because your cat got stuck up a tree, or even if one of your writers has gone missing."

Her cheeks flushed. "Oh, now don't I feel foolish?" But after a moment her blue eyes went hard and she said, "And yet, here you are."

"And yet, here I am, like Jack Nicholson in the *Witches of Eastwick*. I'm here because we do happen to have an interest in Colonel Cameron."

"I bet you have. Maybe some of you are in his book."

The comment annoyed me more than it should have. I smiled without humor. "I doubt it, and as a courtesy I'll refrain from speculating about your private life or assuming you snort coke with champagne-drinking glitteratti." I gave a small shrug. "Given, you know, that stereotypes are anathema and I know nothing about you; and," I added with heavy meaning, "that I am about to ask for your help."

She flushed again and raised her eyebrows. "I'll consider myself told off—for the second time in five minutes! Maybe I should sit down and we can start over."

She moved around the desk and as she sat I asked her, "When was the last time you saw the colonel?"

"Last night. We are celebrating an extended book launch with several events at hotels, major bookstores and other venues. This one was at the Plaza. The great and the good from New York society and the media were there, TV, the press, we even had a Hollywood producer who was interested in the film rights. After dinner Ian got up and gave a talk. He's amazing." She shook her head. "He is a natural showman. Fascinating. He had everybody mesmerized. The man is a goose who will never stop laying golden eggs. I pray that nothing has happened to him."

"Did anything happen during the talk?"

"Nothing special. He made everybody laugh..."

"So how about after the talk? What happened then?"

She shrugged. "He was restless, said he was going to take a walk and smoke a cigarette, maybe have a drink somewhere. I made him promise to be here by eleven this morning, but he never showed up."

"I assume he's usually punctual."

"Very. He's a military man. Discipline is everything. Also his phone has been unobtainable all day. His brother, Alasdair, called me this morning and said he hadn't gone home last night. Apparently, since he's been back in New York he's been very particular about telling his brother where he is and where he is going to be. Alasdair promised to let me know as soon as he showed up, but so far I've heard nothing. Obviously my secretary has phoned around to all the hospitals, but we've drawn a blank. He has vanished off the face of the Earth."

"Obviously you haven't called the cops."

She grinned. "No, I called the Office of the Director of Intelligence Networks instead."

She invited me to smile with her, but I was still sore at her crack about being in the book, so I just narrowed my eyes and looked at the window. Then I told her, "I am going to need a copy of the book. I'll give you a receipt and I'll sign a nondisclosure agreement."

She buzzed her secretary and made arrangements. When she'd finished I said, "I'm almost done, Araminta. I'll get the details from the book. But I have a couple of questions. First, realistically, how much damage is this book going to do, and to what extent can he back it up with proof?"

"Simple answers—a *lot* of damage to some very highly placed people. There will be sackings among senior officials and resignations from both Houses, and from the judiciary. And you can be damn sure there will be resignations. The FBI are going to have a field day. And there will be a public outcry, because this will be a national embarrassment. And proof? Total. I've seen the evidence. He can prove every word."

I nodded. "OK, he must have had a mentor at the CIA, his handler, godfather..."

"Yeah, he names him in the book. General Mike Ustinov. He used to be senator for Texas, he was the chairman of the Committee on Border Control, and a vocal supporter of Trump's wall. He was also governor of Texas for several years, as well as director of the CIA. He has quite a résumé."

"OK." I nodded a few times, thinking. "I'll have to make

some inquiries. I'll get back to you within the next few hours."

Fifteen minutes later, with an advance copy of the colonel's book in my possession, I rose and made my way to the door. With my hand on the handle I stopped and turned to look back at her. She was staring at me and frowning. I said:

"By the way, Ms. Whitley, the Office of the Director of Intelligence Networks you mentioned earlier?" I said, "It doesn't exist."

TWO

Dusk was turning the air to a grainy gray-blue, and all the lights were coming on in the office windows; and the shop fronts, the cafés and the restaurants on 54th Street were all glowing with warm yellow light as I headed for Madison Avenue. East 78th is eastbound only, so I turned left at 79th past the Ukrainian Institute and approached from 5th Avenue.

On East 78th, I stopped outside a neoclassical monster with no less than four columns supporting a balustraded balcony over a marble porch. I double-checked the address Lovelock had sent me, and it was correct. I climbed out of the Cobra and three marble steps led up to the porch where Greco-Roman urns flanked the huge oak double doors set in the granite Tudor arch. A brass button, held in a six-inch brass plate, didn't look very classical or Tudor, but then I guess Plato and Henry VIII didn't use doorbells much. I pressed the brass button and got to wondering about how the ancient Greeks knew if somebody was at the door. I hadn't hit on a satisfactory answer by the time a small hatch set into the big door opened and a small man with nose like a talon peered at me. He didn't say anything so I told him: "My name is Alex Mason, I am here to see Mr. Alasdair Cameron, about his brother."

"Oh," he said, and managed to make it sound Scottish, "Ye'd better come in, then."

He led me across a surprisingly large entrance hall which was framed by a mahogany staircase with a red carpet, that climbed the wall in a square spiral toward the upper floors. A bronze statue of Hermes stood on a pedestal in the center of the floor. He was wearing a winged hat, but he'd forgotten to put on his pants.

He stopped at a set of tall, highly polished walnut doors and knocked, then pushed in without waiting for an answer. I followed before he announced me because I was getting impatient.

The room was long, with two sets of very tall French doors that led out to a large lawn. Light from the lawn lay across burgundy rugs on the floor, cut into distorted squares by the wooden sash bars. The furniture was what you'd expect from two bachelors in their late fifties: a lot of dark wood, red and brown leather, no photographs and no flowers. The smell was of pipe tobacco.

Alasdair Cameron was standing looking out of one of those tall French doors. He must have been six foot three if he was an inch. He was slightly stooped in a Harris tweed suit, and had a shock of very white hair brushed back from a gaunt, boney face. He turned his head to face me, but not like he was in any kind of a hurry. Obviously he didn't see me because he looked right through me and said, "Yes, Lynch?"

His accent wasn't Scottish. It was educated East Coast. Lynch answered like he was giving his boss his most sincere condolences. "Mr. Mason, sir, from Washington."

"Ah." Cameron shifted his gaze to me, like he could now see me, but wouldn't have known I was there unless his butler told him so.

"Mr. Mason, won't you come in? Can I offer you a drink? I generally have a dram before lunch. I understand it is good for the heart. Will you join me?"

"Thank you."

I stepped in and the door closed behind me. I guess Lynch went back to his coffin, and Cameron led me across his Persian rugs to a couple of beaten-up chesterfields arranged beside an old fire. The one on the right had an occasional table beside it with an ashtray, a pipe and a very old hardback edition of *Sense and Sensibility*. I figured that had been his chair since he was eight years old, when he had his first pipe and got hooked on Jane Austen.

I sat in the other chair while he poured whisky from a crystal decanter.

"I gather you are a friend of Araminta Whitley's. I know she has many strings she can pull." He brought two generous measures over in Edinburgh crystal tumblers and handed me one. "I didn't ask you if you wanted ice," he informed me as he folded himself into his chair. Then went on, "I suggested calling the police, but she told me she'd call somebody else in Washington. I assume that was you. Otherwise I'm offering my second best whiskey to the man who's come to read the gas meter." Something like a smile touched the corners of his mouth "*Slàinte!*"

I raised my glass. "*Slàinte!*"

If that was his second best whisky, his best must have been to die for.

"I won't ask you who you represent or what department you work for, Mr. Mason. I have no doubt you'd either lie or tell me to mind my own business. So I will just proceed to tell you what we are dealing with."

"That would be very helpful."

"As I am sure you know, the Gulf Cartel and the Sinaloa Cartel have been rivals for many years, but for many years, culminating some twelve years ago, it was an all-out war that cost tens of thousands of lives all across the north of Mexico, and as far south as Yucatan." He paused to sip. "Of course I say Gulf and Sinaloa, but they were just the two main actors. It drew in the Juarez Cartel, Tijuana, Beltran-Leyva, and of course the Gulf Cartel used the Zatas as their military wing. The estimates are necessarily vague, but some say as many as a quarter of a million people were murdered in that conflict, men, naturally, but also women and children who were frequently killed for the sole purpose of bringing their husbands and fathers to heel. It is no longer all-out war, but neither would it be accurate to say that peace has broken out."

He paused and began to pack a pipe from a leather pouch. "I don't know, Mr. Mason," he said at last, "whether evil is like a weed that grows in suitable conditions, or whether it is a condition that occurs in some human beings.

Be that as it may, I have no doubt at all that the men who run those cartels are evil, in the deepest, simplest, plainest sense of the word. Evil."

I was going to ask him why he was telling me this, but he beat me to the punch.

"I know, you're wondering why on Earth I am telling you this. Well, I have my reasons and if you will bear with me they will become apparent.

"What is not so widely known about the war for supremacy among the cartels in Mexico, is that certain *elements*," he stressed the word as though he was putting inverted commas around it, "certain *elements* of the United States administration had a vested interest in Sinaloa coming out of that conflict on top. Why?"

He arched an eyebrow at me, struck a match and spent a while sucking the flame into the tobacco in his pipe. When he had it spilling thick, aromatic smoke he took it out of his mouth and grunted at it.

"Why...? Because they had friends within the Sinaloa Cartel. In particular Mike Ustinov, who was the director of the CIA at that time, had friends within Sinaloa. So he sent an officer to Mexico to help them. His function, initially, was to liaise between the Sinaloa leadership and the Mexican government, brokering agreements between them. As a part of those deals, the CIA provided the Mexican government with information about Gulf Cartel operations, and, in exchange, the *Federales* allowed Sinaloa shipments to reach the California and Arizona borders unmolested.

"But with time that arrangement developed further. Pretty soon the Mexican government was feeding information to the CIA, so that they could pass it to Sinaloa; information about Gulf Cartel operations so Sinaloa could send men to ambush them and massacre them. Essentially, the Mexican police were using Sinaloa to do their dirty work for them.

"And pretty soon those *elements* I mentioned within our administration began to get wind of the relationship that had developed between the CIA and Sinaloa—and the vast sums of money it was generating for the CIA's black budget funds."

I asked him, "How did that work?"

"Very simply. Sinaloa gave the CIA officer a schedule of shipments: where and when they would cross the border, and in what vehicles. And the CIA would inform customs that X, Y and Z vehicles were part of a CIA operation and must be allowed to pass unmolested. In exchange, and to keep the DEA happy, once a month a shipment was earmarked, the DEA and Border Control were alerted and that shipment was stopped." He gave a small, bitter laugh. "Then it would be all over the news, the DEA or Border Control, or the two working together, had intercepted the biggest haul yet. So many kilos of coke and heroin with a street value of so many millions. Meanwhile, fifteen or twenty times that amount had already sailed through that month.

"We are talking about billions of dollars a year. And everybody from senators to governors, judges and sheriffs, wanted a cut. Everyone who could offer a blind eye to turn, wanted in. 'You want free passage though my state on your way to New York?' 'You want to sell unmolested in my state, or my town or my city?' Evil is contagious, Mr. Mason, and it feeds on greed and power."

His pipe had been burning down and now he puffed at it until it was billowing again. Then he sipped his whisky.

"When stupid, ignorant men get greedy, they think short term about what they can get, about how they can give their appetites immediate gratification. When clever, ambitious men get greedy, they think long-term and they organize. And pretty soon, by the two thousand and teens, the CIA had organized a network of governors, senators, judges and law enforcement officers from San Diego to Blaine and from South Point Texas to Frenchville in Maine, and everything in between, facilitating the import and distribution of marijuana, cocaine and heroin, and various derivatives thereof, nationwide..."

He paused, searching for the right words. "But what was most...most *ingenious* about this setup was the fact that this CIA officer, who had organized all this, had everyone involved believing firmly that they were doing it for patriotic reasons, and they were doing it for the good of the country, for the sake of national security."

"How do you know all this?"

"We'll come to that. Meantime, this network which had been set up was serving a different purpose. It, and the services that the CIA was providing for Sinaloa, were, as I say, generating billions of dollars every year. And the CIA was funneling its share of that money into black ops in other parts of the world where it also had interests; primarily in the Middle East."

"Anti-terrorist operations in fundamentalist Islamic nations?"

He laughed. "Dear me, no. Those operations, whether black ops or not, end up getting a high profile and the funding is from the legitimate defense budget. No, we are talking about such things as selling weapons and equipment to Hamas and Hezbollah, enabling them to fire rockets into our close ally Israel. We are talking about selling weapons to the Taliban and Al-Qaeda, which they used to kill American and allied soldiers—"

I raised a hand. "No, wait, slow down. Why in hell would the American government sell weapons to Islamic terrorists? What possible benefit—"

"To the US Government, none."

I spread my hands. "So?"

He sighed and puffed on his pipe for a moment. "All right, Mr. Mason, bear with me for a moment. Imagine that I am the president of Dystopia. My daughter is the director of the Dystopian Bank and you, her husband, own a tank factory."

I sighed, like I was getting bored. He ignored me.

"I declare war on Utopia, and immediately order a thousand tanks from you. How do I pay? Certainly not from my personal money. After all, it is the office of president that has declared war, not mere Alasdair Cameron. No, I pay for the tanks from the national defense budget, which is drawn from the taxes I levy on the people. The people pay.

"Now, the problem is this: the budget only gets me two hundred tanks, and I need a thousand. So I go to my daughter's bank and I borrow two billion dollars to pay for all the tanks and the ammunition and the food and all the rest of the expenses that I am going to need for my war. She lends me the money which, once interest is added over however many years, is close to a trillion dollars. Where does all that money end up? In my daughter and my son-in-law's bank accounts. Where does it come from? The taxpayer. Has it cost me or my government anything? Absolutely nothing." He shrugged. "So maybe in the real world it is not daughters and son-in-laws who benefit, but it most certainly *is* friends and colleagues, and members of the same club. But my point is that one thing is the national interest, and quite another is the interest of those friends who helped me get into office.

"So, ultimately, it may be very much against America's interest to help Hamas send rockets into Israel, but if Abbu-Abbas-ben-Amini, the leader of Hamas, has a cousin who is part of a particular Islamic royal family, and they are in a position to grant certain oil concessions to my friend Bill who was at Yale with me and, like me, is a member of Skull and Bones, well it might be in *my personal* interest and his. So, as with the war, it's not good for the country, but it is good for my group of friends and family, for my club, my clan."

"You are telling me that members of the United States administration, the CIA, the White House, the Pentagon, law enforcement and the judiciary conspired to use revenue derived from assisting Sinaloa to smuggle drugs into the country, to arm and equip Islamic terrorist groups to attack Israel and fight against US troops, in exchange for personal benefits including oil concessions. That is what you are telling me."

He nodded. "That is exactly what I am telling you, and the prime agents who made it happen were my brother and his handler, General Mike Ustinov, one-time director of the CIA. Israeli civilians have died, men, women and children, murdered with rockets supplied and paid for by this gang of conspirators. American troops have been shot, maimed and killed with bullets, guns and bombs supplied and paid for by this group of conspirators. They don't care if their actions damage the national interest. They care about their own interests, and the interests of their friends."

His pipe had died and he tapped out the ash into his ashtray, where it lay smoldering.

"This is what they call the global economy. Industries and corporations supersede the nation state, and they take your loyalty with them."

I drained my glass and shook my head. "It's a great story, Mr. Cameron, but I am afraid I find it very hard to believe."

"Of course you do." He laughed again, his dry humorless laugh. "Who would believe a story like that? It's part of the genius of the thing. It's like the Bilderberg group. Who is going to believe that Bill Gates, Mark Zuckerberg, King Charles III of England and Elon Musk would meet in secret, with the CEO of Shell and the leading physicists from Oxford and Harvard, to discuss the future of the planet? But they do, every year. The last one was in Washington DC, last June. They discussed geopolitical realignments, NATO, China, Russia, get this, continuity of government and the economy, put that in your pipe and smoke it if you like," he barked a laugh and went on, "They discussed disinformation, the fragmentation of democratic societies, and of course Ukraine."

"Mr. Cameron, I am not so naïve that I believe American law enforcement is immune to corruption. But the scale of what you are suggesting is huge. Somewhere along the line it would have to spring a leak."

"And when it does—as it has—people like you dismiss it and say it isn't possible. Meanwhile, some of the cruelest, most sadistic bastards on the planet are paid to encourage the members not to spring leaks." He shrugged. "But you don't need to believe it, Mr. Mason. You just need to investigate it. My brother was that CIA officer, and in his book, and in his private papers, he has all the proof you will ever need."

THREE

"I have an advance copy of the book," I told Alasdair Cameron. He had stood to pour two more generous measures of whisky.

"That's more than I have," he said.

"But I take it you have his notes, documents, photographs—the proof that his allegations are true."

He made a noise like a loud cough. "Have," he said. "I *have* them in the most elastic sense of the word. I have access to them and, if as I suspect, Ian is dead, then when his death is proved, I will inherit them. I have *possession* of them. But Jesus Christ himself could come down and ask me where they were, and I would not tell him."

He handed me my refill and bent himself into a lanky, crooked N as he sat back in his chair. "However, you can take my word for it, every single allegation in that book is backed up and proved by the documents and photographs, letters and emails that Ian saved over the years and stored away safely. If the time ever comes I can show them to you, but right now I would trust a rattlesnake with a hornet up its ass more than I trust you, or anyone else working for the US Government. Forgive me if that sounds rude, but it is what it is."

I studied my glass and nodded. "In that case I am doubly grateful for your sharing this superb whisky with me. I can understand your lack of trust. I tend to feel pretty much the same way a lot of the time." I thought for a moment and took a deep breath. "Mr. Cameron, right now I am simply assessing the situation. That is as far as my brief goes. But if I understand you, what you would like us to do is, A, find out whether your brother is alive, and, B, if he is not, find out how he died. If it turns out he was murdered, then, C, you would like us to find out who killed him."

"That pretty well sums it up, yes."

We talked some more. I finished my whisky, thanked him for his hospitality and his time and stepped out into the night. The sky was overcast with luminous orange clouds, the floodlit trees in Central Park rustled and sighed, and I made my way slowly down 5th Avenue to the Plaza Hotel, with the hood down and the cool air on my face. Either by design or serendipity, Lovelock had booked me into, as it were, the scene of the crime. If indeed there had been any crime. So when I had handed the car over to the kid from the valet parking, I made my way to the reception desk to have a word with the concierge. He was a dapper man in a blue suit, who looked fifteen years younger than his forty years.

"Were you here last night, at Ian Cameron's book launch?"

"Yes sir, I certainly was."

I showed him my Pentagon ID card. "Did you happen to notice when he left?"

He handed it back with a look that said he had seen far more impressive things in his time. "Why yes, he left right after his talk. It must have been shortly after eleven. I remember because he stopped just outside the hall to light a cigarette. He saw me looking and made a crack about how he had spent his entire life breaking rules. Then he stepped outside and stood at the bottom of the steps smoking for a couple of minutes."

"Did you happen to notice if a car stopped to collect him?"

"No, no, nobody stopped." he shook his head. "After a moment he turned right and started strolling."

I nodded. "That is very helpful. But tell me something, why did you happen to notice that?"

He arched an eyebrow, like he was getting ready to be offended. "Excuse me?"

"Don't get sore. I'm just wondering, there must have been a lot of people around after the launch and the talk, a lot of things going on, the lobby was probably full. I am wondering if anything in particular happened outside to make you notice the colonel smoking, turning right and—"

"Well, as a matter of fact, yes. There was something. Doggy."

"Doggy?"

He shook his head like he was slightly exasperated. "He's harmless, a homeless gentleman who lives in the park and occasionally wanders past the hotel around eleven in the evening, when people are going home after dinner. I think he figures that well fed and after a few glasses of wine, they may be more disposed to give him a few dollars. The police turn a blind eye, but we can't have him bothering our clients on our very doorstep, can we? So we keep an eye on him and if he comes too close we shoo him away."

"He was there last night?"

"Across the road. He has a pram and he wheels a dog around in it."

"Doggy."

"Precisely. I noticed him staring at Colonel Cameron, but the colonel saluted him, turned and walked away, toward Grand Army Plaza."

"I know it would have been hard to tell, but did he strike you as agitated, nervous...?"

He smiled. "The colonel? Not at all. He looked relaxed. He was strolling, like he was enjoying the evening."

I thanked him and stepped out onto the red carpeted steps and stood there a while with my hands in my pockets, thinking that a little less than twenty-four hours earlier the colonel had done something similar. He had stood there, smoking a cigarette. He had seen the homeless guy opposite, tipped him a salute and turned toward 5th Avenue.

I did the same thing, strolling toward the Army Plaza and the Pulitzer fountain, with my hands in my pockets, watching the crowds. There were lots of them, milling, jostling, standing and talking; and there was traffic, lots of that too. So what happened? One thing was certain, he was not killed here on the street. So did he hail a cab and get himself killed elsewhere? Did he meet someone and go off somewhere else with them?

I crossed over to the fountain and stood with my back to it, staring diagonally across West 59th at the park. For a moment I wondered whether Araminta Whitley and the colonel had dreamed the whole thing up as a publicity stunt. It wasn't that hard to believe and in some ways it was the best way it made sense.

I did a slow, three-sixty-degree turn and asked myself what was least likely, a publicity stunt, or a battle-hardened colonel with years of covert combat experience, getting abducted on West 59th Street among hundreds of witnesses. In the end I decided it was even money and crossed over toward the park, intending to look for Doggy.

It turned out he wasn't hard to find. He was the sociable type and liked to approach people and engage them in conversation. Usually it was the kind of conversation which concluded with him asking them for money, but he made them feel he'd given them something in return.

I found him by the horse carriages, near the statue of Thomas Moore. He was probably only in his forties, but he looked old, worn out. He had a long beard down to his belly that didn't make him look any younger, and a hat that made him look like Merlin. He was sitting on a bench and had an old-fashioned pram beside him with a dog sitting in it with a look of permanent worry on its face.

I approached him and sat beside him. He looked away, like I'd embarrassed him somehow. I said, "Are you the guy they call Doggy?"

"I dunno," he said without any teeth. "You're the guy they call what?" and he grinned, in as much as a man with no teeth can grin. I pulled a ten from my wallet and showed it to him. "I'm looking for Doggy to give him this ten-dollar bill. If you're Doggy, tell me before I go look somewhere else."

He nodded with his eyes fixed on the bill. "I'm Doggy. Is that for me?"

"Sure." I gave it to him. "I have another one for you if you'll answer some questions for me."

He stuffed the money inside his old jacket behind his beard and spoke without looking at me.

"Kind of questions?"

"You were here last night?"

"What if I was?"

"Did you take your dog for a stroll over to the Plaza, in his pram?"

"Ain't no harm in that, is there? I can go there. It's public highway if I stay this side of the road. Long as I don't molest the guests on the steps."

"Sure. Listen, I'm not coming after you, Doggy. Didn't I just give you ten bucks?" He nodded and conceded I had. "I am just interested in what you might have seen last night. And if you stop answering my questions with questions of your own, maybe I can give you another ten bucks."

He surprised me by giving his toothless grin again and a short laugh. "I do that," he said. "My way of avoidin' trouble. Never say yes nor no. Someone told me that once. Always answer with a question."

"Well, that's good advice, Doggy, most of the time, but right now it could cost you ten bucks. So tell me, last night, did you see a big guy in a tux standing on the stairs of the Plaza smoking a cigarette?"

He licked his lips a couple of times, nodded and said, "I seen 'im."

"What did he do?"

"He was the colonel. He spoke to me a few times, give

me a smoke, five or ten bucks sometimes. Told me he'd bin in the army, and he was a colonel."

"So did he talk to you last night?"

He shook his head. "Nah, he give me a salute, on account of he was a colonel, and he walked away down t'ord 5th Avenue. I went with him, stayin' this side of the road, hopin' he'd see me and maybe cross over. I like talkin' to him. He had good stories, and he'd always give me some-thin'. I ain't got a job, y'know."

"I understand, Doggy. So you followed him along on this side of the road, while he was walking toward 5th Avenue. And what happened?"

His gaze drifted away toward the water. His voice became vague. He said, "I dunno, really. I think he met some friends."

"Friends? What friends? What did they look like?"

His face became kind of queasy and he shrugged. "I dunno if they was friends, really. I didn't like 'em. They didn't shake hands or nothin'. But the woman seemed to like him."

"A woman?"

He grinned. "She was nice. Red dress, nice figure, she come up to him and he stopped to talk with her. She come up close and put her hands on him, on his chest."

"Could you describe her?"

"Well, they was pretty far away. But she had on that cute red dress, and I think she had a hat on her head. And a real nice figure. Sexy."

He cackled and I laughed with him. They must have been forty yards apart, and any detail at that distance and at night would have been impossible to make out.

"So they talked. Did they talk for long?"

"Not long, just kind of, 'Hey, how ya doin', blah blah,' kinda thing. Then the other friends showed up."

"OK, so she showed up first and then the other guys showed up."

"It all kinda happened at the same time. You gonna pay me, right?"

"You know I am, but keep going."

"OK, so when she's comin' up close with him a black van pulls up and three guys climb out, like they was drivin' past and saw him and stopped to say hello. I figured maybe they was old army buddies."

"They climb out and what do they do?"

"They climb out and they go over to him and the woman."

"OK, this is great, Doggy. Now I want you to think and tell me exactly how you remember it. Where did they stand?"

He stared at me a moment like I was nuts, then frowned. "Well, well they stood behind him. That's weird, right? They stood behind him and then him and the woman, and one of the guys got in the van, and the other two got up front and drove away, east."

"Nobody else spoke to them, or hassled them or tried to stop them?"

"No, no they just got in, nice and easy, and drove away."

I gave him a twenty, thanked him and told him to stay safe. Then I made my way back to the hotel. In my room I called Nero.

"Well?"

"He has been abducted. He was abducted right here on

59th Street and 5th Avenue, by a beautiful woman in a red dress and three men in a dark SUV. His handler and mentor seems to have been General Mike Ustinov. He is one of a large number of people who will suffer great pain when the book is published."

"I know him. The man is barely human, but he is intelligent. And killing Colonel Cameron at this stage serves little purpose. On the contrary, it would be counterproductive."

I sighed. "Yeah, unless..."

"Unless pressure is then brought to bear on the publisher to kill the publication or heavily edit the book. But again, at this very late stage, that is extremely unlikely. If anyone were to attempt that they would have done it months ago."

"What do you want me to do?"

"Go to Texas, talk to that revolting man, make him understand that you are there to *help* him. This is a club, a clan, we all stand to lose as a result of this book, yadda yadda... You understand."

"I understand."

I was going to hang up but he stopped me. "Alex?"

"Yes sir?"

"I want Colonel Ian Cameron. His book will take care of all his bloody associates, but it will make a hero of him. I don't want that to happen. I want him to foot the bill for what he has done."

"Yeah, I want that too. I'm going to read the book. In the morning I'll head for Texas."

"Good. Keep me informed."

I called room service for a hamburger and a couple of cold beers, stretched out on the bed and opened the book.

There was an introduction which, it turned out, Cameron had written himself. It started:

GUILT, repentance, remorse and regret. Each one is slightly different, and each one serves its own purpose. Regret is the least dynamic of the four and is simply a state where we wish we had not done something, or that something had not happened. Remorse is like regret on steroids. That is when you really wish you hadn't done something, so much that it hurts. In addition, remorse has religious overtones and maybe, on your deathbed, you are already feeling the heat of the burning pokers they're about to shove up your ass. Repentance is, for me, the noblest of the four, because as well as carrying all the meaning of regret, it also speaks of a determination to set things right, or at least to do what you can to mitigate the harm you have done. And finally guilt. Guilt is a mental and emotional paralysis invented by the Judeo-Christian religions to keep their drones obedient and pliant... Let it be said, right from the start, that I feel none of the above.

THIS, I told myself, was going to be an interesting read. Ian Cameron, assuming he was still alive, was clearly some piece of work.

FOUR

Colonel Ian Cameron was still alive. He was half-lying, half-sitting on a cast-iron bed that was probably a couple of hundred years old. He had his hands cuffed to the bedstead. The walls of the room had once been white, probably around the time the bed was installed. Now they were the color of tired briefs that had been worn too often and not washed often enough. The ceiling, for some reason known only to the guy who did it, had been painted yellow. Maybe it had seemed like a good idea at the time. Or maybe the decorator was out of his mind on peyote.

Sweat trickled down the colonel's cheek. Unconsciously he raised his shoulder as though to wipe it away. Overhead a fan creaked rhythmically, in a listless tribute to Mexican economic genius: The electricity got used to move the fan, it failed to cool the air but that didn't matter because the meter was fixed anyway so the electricity never got paid. A sash window with peeling paint overlooked a dusty square. A squat church glared white against the blue sky.

The two guys who had come with them were down in the hotel bar having a beer and something to eat. The woman was sitting on a bentwood chair at the foot of the bed. She was in jeans and a white shirt, with walking boots on her feet. She looked fresh and cool, and Cameron wanted very badly to kill her. She said:

"Samuel Mariano Zamora."

"What about him? How long have I been out?"

"A long time. Hours. You two were pals."

"Yeah, we were real close. Where the hell are we?"

She studied his face a moment, like she was deciding whether to tell him or not. Finally she said, "Rosario, fifty miles north of Obregon, three hundred miles northwest of Culiacan."

"That's on the borders of Sonora. You're out of your mind." He shook his head. "You don't know what you're up against."

"Maybe. Maybe that's why I brought you along. Stop stalling, Colonel. Let's talk about Zamora."

He swallowed. "Talk about him?" He barked an unpleasant laugh. "What's to talk about? He is a very dangerous man. He owns the Mexican government. He owns part of the United States government, for Christ's sake! I mean..." He looked at the window, shook his head. "What are you...?" He concluded the question with another shake of his head.

The woman sighed. "Keep pushing, Colonel, and I will detonate the charge in your back. But there is a lot I can do before we get to that." She held his eye and blinked a couple of times before going on. "We are both professionals. We have both been taught, if you are going to interrogate someone, show the subject you are ready and willing to go the extra nine yards. Prove to them that you are willing to go beyond that point where normal people turn back. We were both taught that, right?"

He didn't answer. He swallowed.

"I have not done that with you, Colonel. Yet. Because when I take you back home, I would rather there was not a scratch on you. But if I have to show you that I am serious, I can call Dave right now and tell him to bring the tool kit from the car."

"No."

It was a short, dry statement.

She sat forward with her elbows on her knees. "Colonel, do I need to prove to you that I mean business?"

"No."

"Piss me around, try to play me, get smart on me like you just did? Do that again, and I will give you no warning and no chance of appeal. I will cut through bone, with no anesthetic. Do you understand me?"

"Yes."

"Zamora."

"He's the head of the Sinaloa Cartel. He has houses all over northern and eastern Mexico. There are plenty of photographs of him, when he was younger, but he had plastic surgery a few years back and only his closest associates know what he looks like now. So he keeps moving and he keeps a low profile, so he never gets caught."

He paused, trying to read her face. She said nothing, did nothing, just waited, so he went on.

"Truth is, Mexican law enforcement won't touch him because the Company—the CIA—"

"I know who the Company is."

"So, they sent word that Zamora was not to be touched."

"Tell me about the arms deals."

He grunted. "That started when Mike Ustinov was director of the CIA. Iran was suffering reduced gas and oil sales because of sanctions, but they were cooperating with Qatar in developing the South Pars field. It's the biggest field in the world and it's in Iran's territorial waters in the Persian Gulf. They share the field with Qatar.

"So Mike figures, OK, Iran run its own wells through various nationalized oil companies, and its oil production and sales were also practically crippled by international sanctions. So from that perspective that was a bad time to get into Iranian oil production. However, seen from a different angle, that was a *perfect* time to take any kind of offer to Iran, because they were suffering badly, and their cooperation with Qatar provided an open door to anyone who might otherwise have been excluded from working with the Iranian nationalized oil industry. You still with me?"

"I am still with you."

"So, pulling strings in Qatar, Mike managed to arrange several meetings with Iranian officials. They were willing to grant concessions to American companies to supply drilling equipment, exploration rights and other concessions in field development and refining, and Qatar was more than willing to help blur the US involvement, but Iran insisted on one thing. They wanted weapons, and particularly rockets, rocket parts and rocket-targeting technology to be supplied to Hezbollah, in Beirut, so that they could target Israel. Without that condition being satisfied, there was no deal."

"So what was Zamora's involvement?"

He sighed. Overhead the fan squeaked. Outside the window there was only the heavy, still silence of midday heat.

"You're not going to believe it. I don't know who you work for, but you are not going to believe what I am going to tell you."

"Try me."

"Zamora sends a message to his pal, General Luis Sanchez, at SEDENA, the *Secretaría de la Defensa Nacional*, or the Department of Defense to you and me, and tells him to order I can't remember how many quidzillion FGM-148 Javelin surface-to-surface rockets complete with infrared homing devices—heat seekers—from the States."

"How many?"

He puffed out his cheeks. "Uh, it's in my book. I can't remember the exact number, but it was a couple of thousand or more. So he tells him to place the request via Senator Walther Gannett, who is a pal of Mike's, to fast track it because it's for use in a campaign against the Gulf Cartel. Still with me?"

"Yeah. Zamora tells Sanchez to order several thousand surface-to-surface missiles via Senator Gannett, pretending they are to be used against the Gulf Cartel."

"Right. So the rockets are duly sent to the *Base Aérea Militar* Number Ten. I will give you only one guess as to where that military air base is located."

"Culiacán, in Sinaloa."

"The *capital* of Sinaloa. The rockets were offloaded, the United States Air Force transport departed and a convoy of trucks left the base to carry the rockets to various locations on the East Coast. Unfortunately the convoy was hijacked, or so the story goes, though there were no witnesses left alive to tell the story. A couple of days later those rockets turned up in Tehran, and shortly after that, confidential reports from the Mossad complained to the Pentagon that American-made FGM-148 Javelin surface-to-surface rockets were being fired into Israel by Hezbollah.

"A few months after that, the Zeta Cartel suffered a crippling attack from government forces assisted by CIA officers, and the DEA stated, in a confidential report to Congress, that there had been a fifteen percent increase in cocaine and heroin on the streets of the United States."

"The drugs had been waved through as their payment for the deal."

"That was the deal."

"You brokered it."

"Largely. I was the man in the middle, running back and forth with messages. 'He'll do A if you'll get Z to do X.'"

"A lot of innocent people in Israel died so that Mike Ustinov and Walther Gannett could secure oil concessions for their masters."

"Yeah." He nodded. He looked serious. "I heard that by the end of this century, in the next eighty years, around eight thousand million—that's eight billion people—will die. Not because of wars, or nuclear strikes, or famine or global warming or any other shit. Today they are alive, and in eighty years most of them will be dead. That's how it works."

"Are you still in touch with Zamora?"

His eyes shifted involuntarily to his cell on the table by the window. "I mean, not for a while..."

Something changed in her face. Something died in her eyes, like she was folding away her humanity so it wouldn't get stained by what she was about to do.

"No!" he said it and then shouted it, trying to pull in his legs. "*No, no!* Yes, I can be in touch. I have his number, I can call him. He'll be glad to hear from me. Hell!" He laughed. "We were like brothers! Yeah, I can be in touch with him."

"Good. Do this right, and you get to live. You understand that? Screw it up, warn, advise, suggest, imply *anything* at all to him and I will blow your spine in half."

"I get it, I get it. I know you're serious. You don't need to prove it."

"A bar, a restaurant, a café, some place where you can meet like old buddies. Preferably not too upmarket. If it's seedy and rough that's better. A place for the guys. You reading me?"

"Yeah, yeah, we used to meet in a few places like that. El Don Felipe, in Pericos, Los Chingados, in Choix..."

"Yeah, I don't need a list. I just need you to choose one. Then you call him and you tell him you want to meet."

"You're out of your mind."

"Where did you most often meet, Colonel?"

"At his villa outside La Campana. It's twenty miles northwest of Culiacán. That's where we met, or sometimes he'd come to my hotel." She stared at him with no expression. He swallowed a couple of times, then exploded, "Look! I'm telling you the truth! He—"

"You said, 'Yeah, yeah, we used to meet in a few places like that. El Don Felipe, in Pericos, Los Chingados, in Choix...'"

"Yeah, OK, I said that, but—"

"I get that you're scared of what Zamora can do to you if he gets suspicious."

"You're not kidding! What I have seen that man do—"

"But right now you need to be very scared of what I *will* do if I get mad. And I am getting mad. I have warned you twice. I will not warn you a third time."

She pulled her cell from her pocket and pressed a single number. After a moment she said, "David, bring the box of tools up."

She hung up and put her cell back in her pocket. The colonel had gone a pale yellow waxy color. His eyes were moist. "What are you doing?"

"Next time I won't warn you. Next time I will remove a digit. And I won't cut through the joint, Colonel. I hope you have finally understood me."

She stood and went to the table behind her. There she poured a shot of Scotch into a glass and carried it, along with the colonel's cell, to the bedside table. She unlocked his right hand and gave him the drink.

"Knock it back." He did as she said and she asked him, "You need another?"

He nodded and she went and refilled the glass. As she handed it to him the door opened and David came in carrying a toolbox. She jerked her head at the table and said, "Stay."

The colonel gave her the empty glass. She said, "OK?"

He nodded. "Give me the phone."

As she handed him the cell she said to David, "Get the pliers."

The colonel stared at her. "That's not necessary."

"In case."

"It's not necessary."

She studied his face a moment, then nodded. "OK."

He took a couple of deep breaths and started to scroll through his address book. After a moment he selected a number and put the phone to his ear. He turned slightly away from her and the woman stepped back, so she was out of his line of vision. She knew if he was going to be natural, for the next minute or so he had to forget about her and believe whatever story he was going to tell Zamora.

Suddenly his face lit up. "Hey, cabrón, how you doin'? Blast from the past, man!"

He laughed a lot as he listened. Then he said, "I'm here, in Mexico. Yeah, I came to see some old girlfriends and I wanna tell you about my book, *hijo puta!*" He laughed out loud. "There is gonna be some weepin' and a moanin' and *wailin'* in DC, man! There are going to be some very unhappy people!" He was quiet for a moment, then, "Nah, nah, nah, nah, no way, bro, you know me better than that. And *I* know *you* better than that. The only people who get hurt in this show are the bad guys. I know they've gone back on their promises. I know they got tough on the border after they said it was secure. They gotta be punished..." He paused a moment. "You listen to me, man, they think because they are north of the border, surrounded by their security services, they can do whatever they like. When this book hits the stands, they are gonna know they are not safe."

He laughed some more, then, "Listen to me. You know what I have been dreaming about? You know the burritos that guy used to make, what was his name? Miguelito! That's the guy! Bar Don Felipe, we used to meet there in Pericos, you remember? And a couple of cold beers. I don't know what he did to that beer, but it was the best beer in town...."

He listened for a minute, smiling like it was all real, nodding. "Man, I would love that. I been sitting in New York and London, watching the rain, locked in my office, dreaming about Mexico. I am telling you, man, next year I am going to retire to Mexico. We gonna be neighbors, dude... Yeah, let's do it. Tomorrow, we'll meet at Bar Don Felipe, we'll have some burritos and cold, cold beer, then we go back to your place and *par-tay*!" He laughed a lot, then told him, "Love you, man! See you tomorrow, twelve noon."

He hung up and his face changed and went gray. He handed the phone to the woman.

"I don't know what you're planning. But if it goes south, please don't let them take me. Shoot me." He looked up at her and there was terror in his eyes. "No one, not even a bastard like me, deserves what they would do to me."

She nodded. "OK."

FIVE

It was raining in DC. It wasn't cold, but it was raining steadily and there was a general, background hiss in the streets, wherever you went. I was in a cab, having left the Cobra in New York, feeling pretty sure I would be back soon. I had caught the early morning train and was now on my way, through heavy, gray drizzle, to the Ritz Carlton on 22nd Street. The nerds at ODIN had managed to track down General Mike Ustinov, erstwhile governor of Texas and ex-director of the CIA, onetime senator for the Lone Star State, and chairman of the Committee on Border Control. Now a prime target for Colonel Ian Cameron.

It had not been hard to find him. He was not in Texas, he was in DC and making no effort not to be found. I got the impression from reading his file that he was the kind of man who came looking for you if he heard you were looking for him. I had called and got his secretary, and she had put me through directly. His reaction had been what you might expect.

"What took you so long?"

I hadn't been able to think of a smart-ass reply, so I got right to the point instead.

"May I come and see you, sir? I'd like to ask you a few questions about Colonel Ian Cameron."

"I'm at the Ritz Carlton in DC. I used to stay at the Hay Adams, but there are too many goddamn politicians there. I bread cattle, and the stink of bullshit is more than I can bear. Then I used to stay at the St. Regis, till they called the street Black Lives Matter Plaza. You know they pedestrianized the goddamn road and wrote 'black lives' all along the street in letters forty-six feet high. Did you know that? Hell, George Washington didn't get that honor! Politics, bullshit. Makes me sick. What did you say your name was?"

"Alex Mason, sir."

"Time it right, I'll buy you lunch."

I guess I timed it right. The driver pulled into the entrance at twelve noon on the button. There he stopped and squinted at me in the mirror, like a man peering into a parallel universe he doesn't really believe exists.

"*Thamaniat dularat,*" he said.

"What?"

He jerked his chin at the mirror, indicating my reflection, and said, "*Ant tadfae li! Thamaniat dularat!*"

I looked at the meter. It said fifteen dollars. I gave him an Abe Lincoln and a Hamilton and told him to have a nice day. He muttered something in Orkish and drove away.

The dedicated concierge told me that the general was in THE suite, which meant he was in the Ritz Carlton suite, which was bigger and better than all the other suites, including the Presidential suite.

I rode the elevator to the top floor and his pretty PA led me through lots of elegant beige and gray out to a large terrace where he had a couple of weights machines set up under an awning. He was working his pectorals when I arrived, grunting and sweating in a gray string-sleeved vest and black tracksuit pants. I figured he was in his late fifties but in good shape. He was stocky, but most of his bulk was muscle. His hair was mainly stubble, and I could see it glistening with droplets of sweat.

He ignored me as he grunted his way toward two hundred and his PA asked me if I would like a drink. I told her I wouldn't and sat. One hundred and ninety-five through to two hundred elicited red-faced shouts rather than grunts, and then he did two hundred and one just for pigheadedness. On that one his neck swelled and his face turned purple.

He released the weights with a loud clatter and sat panting and saying, "Yeah...yeah...yes sir..." Then he rubbed his face with a towel and looked at me. "You Mason?"

"I am."

"You're here about that asshole Cameron?"

"I'd like to ask you some questions about him and his work in Mexico."

"Finally got himself killed, huh?" He stood and stripped off his shirt, his tracksuit pants and his sports shoes, leaving only his shorts. Then he walked over to a couple of buckets he had standing by the wall. I hadn't seen them before but now saw they were filled with water and ice. Without pause he picked one of them up and poured the freezing liquid over his head, roaring as he did so. Then he did the same with the other bucket.

He came back, toweling his head. "Come on, I'm going to get dressed, then we'll have lunch."

His pretty PA and I followed him to the bedroom where he stripped naked and she started handing him clothes. As he pulled on his socks he was saying, "I always liked Ian. He was a tough son of a bitch. His trouble was he had no ideology." He glanced at me. "You understand that?"

I nodded and his pretty PA handed him a pair of Y-fronts from a fresh pack. He pulled them on and she handed him a gleaming white shirt.

"He had no principles. You know, I always thought, a man with no principles is just a smart animal. And that's what Ian is. He's a smart animal. Me? I read philosophy, physics, literature..."

She handed him some well-tailored gray woolen pants. He climbed into them.

"I kill a man," he said as he pulled up the zipper, "I send in a troop to clear a village, bomb a town, whatever. I do it for America, for freedom, for democracy. These are things I believe in. See? I know people laugh at all that these days, but they can laugh because they have men like me watching their backs. And when I say men like me, I mean men who are driven intelligently by ideology."

He had done up his belt and slipped on his shoes, and Pretty PA was tying his laces for him while he selected a deep purple tie with tiny gold rhomboids on it. The son of a bitch was elegant and had good taste. As he stood in front of the mirror tying a discrete four-in-hand he kept talking.

"Ideology is not important, Mason. It is more than fundamental. It is essential—OK baby, that's fine. Get me my jacket."

This last was addressed to Pretty PA. She helped him on with the jacket and he kept right on going as he made for the door.

"I say essential because social morals, and that is what ideology is if you take half a second to think about it, social morals are hardwired into human beings. We are social animals. And any man like Ian who has not developed social morals is, like I said at the beginning, nothing more than a smart animal. Let's eat."

In the elevator going down he told me, "I talk a lot. You want to ask me questions, you're going to have to cut in. I do it because I like to be in control, and I think real fast."

The elevator stopped and we stepped out into the lobby. He was still talking. "We'll go to Chet the Chef's on M Street. It's a short walk but we'll go in the Bentley. I don't feel all that safe walking around these days. I eat a lot of protein to keep me in shape. Generally I start with salmon and then a good sirloin steak. Can you live with that?"

The Bentley was parked outside and his chauffeur held the door for us as we climbed in. I sat opposite him where I could see his face. As the driver got behind the wheel up front, behind the soundproof partition, the general drew breath. I beat him to it and said, "General?"

"Yuh—"

"Shut up."

He closed his mouth, tilted his head on one side and frowned at me. I said:

"Quit bullshitting me. It makes you look like you're trying to hide something. You don't need to hide anything from me. I am here to help you. If they thought you were a problem they'd have had Cobra eliminate you. So shut up and let me ask my questions."

"The last person to tell me to shut up was my father. I was fourteen. I broke his nose."

The car eased out of the hotel forecourt and turned north onto 22nd Street. It was silent and smooth and smelt of leather and furniture polish.

"How did you meet Colonel Cameron?"

"That was when I was director of the CIA. I had a few résumés that had been passed up to me because I was hand-selecting personnel for a unit I wanted to get active in Mexico."

"When you say, 'get active,' what does that mean exactly?"

"Well, hell! What does it mean? It means get active, that's what it means. It means what it says!"

"General..." He sighed and grunted and looked away. "Will you answer the question please? In this context, what, precisely, does 'get active in Mexico' mean?"

The Bentley was easing to a halt outside a clinical-looking restaurant on the corner of M Street and 22nd. It had a piece of the sidewalk sectioned off behind artificial green hedges, with tables under parasols. The driver climbed down and opened the door for us. Before he got out General Ustinov looked at me and said, "Do you know why the Soviet Union eventually collapsed?"

He climbed out before I could answer, strode across the sidewalk and pushed through the steel and glass doors into the restaurant. He knew what table he wanted and made directly for it, without waiting for the maître. I followed and sat opposite him. The tablecloth was extremely white, as were the linen napkins. He shook his out with his left hand and dropped it on his lap. I said:

"They were terrified that Maggie Thatcher would attack them with her handbag."

"That's what I call facetiousness."

"Thank you. It's a gift that comes naturally to me."

"Over one third of their national budget was going on defense. Now I believe in the armed forces, Mr. Mason, but no country can afford to spend thirty to thirty-five percent of their budget on defense. So that means, in a country like ours, the armed forces need to generate wealth which they can then use to supplement their budget. What does that mean? It means you march into a country like Iraq and you take control of their oil, you march into a country like Germany, you take control of their heavy industry."

The waiter was standing beside us. He gave us two menus but the general said, "Two martinis, dry, salmon salad to start with, and a glass of the house white, sirloin steak, medium rare for the main course with a glass of your house red. That's for both of us."

The waiter bowed and walked away. I sighed.

"But that is not what happens. Private interests take the spoils of war these days..."

"Right. But I was looking at the enormous wealth cocaine and heroin were generating in Colombia first, and then Mexico. They had the government by the balls. You were either with them, in which case you made a lot of money, or you were against them, in which case you and your family were killed. These guys *really* understood how this damn show works."

"Let me talk for a moment, will you?"

"Shoot."

"So you're looking at the setup in Mexico and Colombia. At that time Colombia rules the roost with billion-dollar exports of cocaine to the United States and Europe."

"Right."

"And you can see that the Mexican cartels are vying with each other to shift comparatively small amounts of marijuana and heroin."

"Correct."

"So you select the strongest and best placed of the cartels, Sinaloa, and you send in a team, headed by Colonel Ian Cameron, to help Sinaloa take control of the market and at the same time block access to the United States from Colombia, so all Colombian exports have to go through Mexico. You take a very large slice of the profits and thus you fund your personal armed forces."

"Well done, you understood it. The collateral benefit is that the trade, though in itself repugnant, obeys Darwin's law of evolution by helping to cull the weakest and the poorest elements of the race."

The waiter brought the martinis. He sipped, smacked his lips and sighed. I said:

"When the colonel's book hits the stands, the FBI will have to investigate you. There will probably be a congressional inquiry. You will probably spend the rest of your life in prison."

He laughed. "The way Oli North did?"

"That was a somewhat different situation, General. In that case the proceeds of arms sales were diverted to an army which was fighting to stop the spread of Communism in Central America. What you are talking about is the Central

Intelligence Agency assisting a drugs cartel in exchange for billions of dollars, which the CIA held onto to fund its own operations."

"That's right, Mr. Mason. And when that book is published, one of two things will be true. Either he can prove it or he can't. If he can't prove it, then he and his publisher and Congress along with them, can go and screw themselves. If they can prove it, then I will reveal what those black operations were that we used those funds for, and there will not be a red-blooded American in this great country of ours that will not applaud our actions."

"You believe that?"

"I know it to be true."

"In the minds of most Americans, red-blooded or otherwise, what kind of operation is going to justify flooding the country with drugs?"

He smiled. "Why, anti-terrorist operations, of course."

"General, did you order Colonel Ian Cameron killed?"

He frowned, like my stupidity confused him. "Why in hell would I do a dumb-ass thing like that? I want that bastard alive so I can put him on the stand and have my lawyers have a feeding frenzy with him. He may have documentary proof of every order I gave him and other things beside, but in this great jury system we have in this country, victory comes down to two things: how good a showman is your attorney, and how good is he at making the jury understand the *context* in which you did what you did? Can he make them think, 'I would have done the same thing if I had been in his place.' That, that little phrase? That is forgiveness, my friend." He shrugged as the waiter laid two salmon salads in front of us. "I campaigned for Trump's wall. Now I ask you," he said, picking up his fork, "is that the action of a hypocrite? Or is it the action of a patriot, forced to make an unholy alliance in order to protect his country, and doing what he can to protect his country in the process? Take your pick." He stabbed a slice of salmon. "I think my track record, if I ever have to publish it, will speak for itself."

SIX

We finished the salad in silence and he drained his glass of white wine. As he set down the glass I asked him:

"OK, so you would have no reason to abduct or eliminate Colonel Cameron. What about his Mexican contacts in Sinaloa?"

He bunched up his mouth, shrugged his shoulders and shook his head, all at the same time. "What do they care? They are among the world's most wanted men anyway. What's the book going to do, say, hey, the worst criminals in the world cooperated with CIA agents and members of Congress and the judiciary? That's not a problem for them, it's a feather in their cap. It adds to their charisma of power. Besides—"

He leaned back to allow the waiter to put a plate of steak in front of him. He placed another in front of me and the wine waiter poured a couple of glasses of claret. When they'd gone he went on.

"Ian made some good friends out there. People have very stereotypic ideas about the people in the narco business, but let me tell you. They know more about loyalty than any pampered fairies and fags up on the Hill, or in the White House. Believe me—" He picked up his knife and fork and cut into his steak. The blood oozed out and mixed with the oil on the plate. "The worst vengeance you will ever face is that of a Mexican drug dealer. They are out of control and have no inhibitions at all. But if he once takes you as a member of his clan, or his family, that guy will die for you and not bat an eyelid. I have seen that with my own eyes. And Zamora and Ian became real close buddies. I can't see Ian screwing Zamora, or Zamora getting too upset about the book. On the contrary. He probably thinks it's a gas."

I picked up my knife and fork, sighed and laid them down again. "General, few people know Colonel Cameron better than you do."

"That's probably true."

"And I would imagine that few people know his enemies as well as you do."

"Also true."

"Sir, hazarding a guess, who do you think has abducted, or killed, Colonel Cameron?"

He didn't hesitate.

"Nobody. I think this is a classic Ian stunt. He whips up a lot of press and speculation about the book. The book makes this claim and that claim and he can prove it, heads will roll on the Hill, in the Pentagon, blah blah blah. And then he gets abducted. It's all over the news, in the papers, social media is buzzing with it, pre-sales of his book skyrocket, and then he reappears having heroically escaped. That is Ian all over. The man is a scoundrel."

I thought back to Doggy's description of how he had been met by the woman and taken into the van, no fight, no struggle, no plea for help...

"Right now," the general was saying, "he is probably in Mexico, at Ismael Zamora's villa, or with his second in command, Francisco Gallardo, snorting coke, partying with beautiful Mexican babes, having the time of his life. He'll surface in about a month, a very rich man, regarded by most Americans as a hero. I'd lay money on it."

It was a depressingly likely scenario.

I ate half the steak and pulled off half the glass of wine, then leaned back and said: "Put me in touch with Zamora. Talk to him, arrange a meeting for me."

He thought about it for a couple of seconds, then shrugged. "Why should I?"

"I can think of a few reasons. First, if you do, when *Sex Drugs and Rock 'n' Roll at the White House* hits the bookstores, if you need backup to keep you out of prison, ODIN can pull some very significant strings on your behalf."

He made a face like he wasn't all that impressed. I went on.

"Second, the converse is true. If you don't, when the book hits the stands we can make damn sure you get to see the inside of a high-security jail for a nice long stretch. Maybe not the rest of your life, but certainly long enough to impress a few lifers with your firm abs and pecs."

I grinned and he arched an eyebrow. The stakes were getting higher.

"You've met Nero. You know he is more than able.

Third, if you don't, I will personally put your name forward to Cobra. You are just the kind of soulless murdering bastard they specialize in."

He laughed. "Cobra? That's a myth put out by the CIA. Those hits were military hits carried out by Delta or the British SAS."

I smiled. "Shall we find out? Or would you rather do your patriotic duty?"

He sighed. "OK, I'll call the embassy out there. You know Bill Ortega? He's the CIA attaché out there."

"Yeah, I know Bill."

He considered me for a moment, then added, "I'll be staying at my place in Calgary for a couple of months. I like hunting in the mountains up there. But my secretary will be in touch."

"Thanks for lunch."

I stepped out into the rain. It had progressed from steady drizzle to actual rain and seemed to be aspiring for promotion. I hunched my shoulders, hailed a cab and as I climbed in, told him to take me to Wilson Boulevard in Arlington.

"Das ova da riva," he told me. It was obviously Brilliant Taxi Driver Day on planet Earth.

"Yeah, it's over the river," I told him back, wiping my face and my hair with my handkerchief.

"I know."

I looked in the mirror, saw him watching me and decided to ignore him. I called Nero.

"Alex—"

"Sir, I want to come in and report."

"Now?"

"I'm in a cab on my way."

"I have two dozen Coffin Bay king oysters and a bottle of perfectly chilled *Chevalier-Montrachet Grand Cru—Les Demoiselles 2018—Louis Jadot...*"

I gazed out at the rain for a moment and sighed. He was waiting for me to say I'd take a walk around the park while he had lunch. Instead I said, "Well, that is extremely generous of you, sir. I've already had lunch but I am sorely tempted to accept. I'll see you in twenty minutes."

By the time I got there and walked into his office he had finished the oysters and was mopping up the sauce with hunks of baguette. He still had some wine left, but it was all in his glass. He turned his hand up and gestured at the debris on his desk as I sat down. "You took so long," he said simply and shrugged.

"It's OK," I told him. I had already eaten.

"Good, then we'll have some coffee, and perhaps a glass of Armagnac." He pressed the buzzer on his desk. "Lovelock, bring in the *Château de Pellehaut* and a couple of suitable glasses." He didn't wait for an answer but settled back in his chair and released something between a sigh and a grunt. "So, Alex, are we wasting our time on Colonel Cameron, or is there something of import here?"

"It is possible we are wasting our time. I've just had a talk with General Mike Ustinov. In his opinion Cameron has set this whole thing up as a publicity stunt to sell more books."

Another soft grunt. "Evidence for such a view?"

The door opened and the exquisite Lovelock came in with a bottle of forty-year-old Armagnac and two suitable cut crystal glasses. She left them on the desk, winked at me and departed, leaving a hollow feeling behind her. Nero poured, and arched an eyebrow as he poured.

"Lust clouds the mind, Alex."

We sipped and as I set down the glass I told him, "Just about everybody he ever came in contact with has reason to want him dead. I say just about because there are a couple of notable exceptions, and those are the top brass of the Sinaloa Cartel, with whom apparently he has a good relationship. Everybody else, from the CIA top brass, to members of Congress and the executives of several administrations, might be very happy to see Colonel Ian Cameron given his marching orders to the halls of fire and brimstone,"

"Very visual."

"But—"

He interrupted me with a languid voice and his eyes half-closed, "But it would avail them naught, it would be a great risk and serve only to lend credibility to the book's allegations. Not only that, it would boost sales and make their crimes even more widely known, and seriously prejudice any tribunals they may eventually have to face. However, your earlier point, which you failed to make, was that the only people who are not affected by these considerations, and have the wherewithal to execute his abduction and his possible murder, have neither the need nor the desire to do so. I refer of course to Sinaloa and Ismael Mario Zamora García."

"Thank you, sir." I hid my irritation behind my glass and sipped some of the sublime amber liquid. "I could not have put it better myself."

"I am quite certain of that." He refilled us both.

"So, sir, why do we care?"

Nero very rarely smiled because he had no sense of humor. When he did it was an interesting thing to observe. It was a kind of displacement of his jowls back toward his ears, and his eyes became hooded and slightly abstracted.

"That is actually a good question, Alex."

"Just occasionally, sir."

"You are not one hundred percent convinced that this is a publicity stunt."

"No, that is true, sir."

"What is it, precisely, that makes you doubt?"

I thought about it for a moment. "The abduction itself."

"You found witnesses?"

"Yes." I told him what I had learned at the hotel. He listened with his eyes closed, and at the end I concluded, "I know it doesn't make a lot of sense but, it was not violent enough to be a stunt." He nodded. "If it was a stunt, he would want people to notice. He would want lots of witnesses. He would have men in balaclavas wrestling him into the car. This guy has lived with violence all his life, plus he is a natural showman—his publisher told me that. He would want the abduction to be noticed. But the people who took him were trying *not* to be noticed. They were three men and a woman, dressed normally, with no visible weapons, and they quietly guided him to the SUV and he climbed in." I shrugged. "He didn't do that because he was trying to get noticed, he did that because he feared for his life and thought his best option was to do as he was told."

He nodded. "Faultless reasoning, Alex. Now take it a step further." I frowned. He waited. I frowned some more. He sighed. "We have just concluded, have we not, that those who would wish to abduct him and murder him cannot, and those who can do not wish to. Yet we have also concluded that his abduction is not a stunt. So this leaves us with a large, yawning question..."

"Who the hell took him?"

He planted an expression of self-satisfied smugness on his jowls and said, "And that is why we care. We want to know who has taken him, and above all we want to know what their motivation is. In precisely what way is Colonel Ian Cameron a threat to these people?"

His reasoning made a lot of sense. There was just one problem. I didn't have a single lead to follow.

"I have a dark SUV, three men and a woman, probably pros."

"Unquestionably professionals."

"All right, unquestionably professionals. I have nothing else."

"You have read his book?"

"Of course, and I have access to his notes, photographs, documents et cetera through his brother, but he demands ironclad assurances that they will not be spirited away and disposed of."

"Understandable. You found nothing in the book?"

"On the contrary. The book substantiates the hypothesis that it's a stunt."

"Quite. Well, that leaves us with one avenue where we might find a vein of information, if you will forgive the mixed metaphor."

"I'll try. What avenue is that?"

He picked up his glass and held it up so that the light from the window shone through the pale, amber liquid. His passed it beneath his nose and sipped, then replaced the glass on his desk while licking his lips.

"Alex, it is self-evident. What other avenue lies open to you? You have said yourself that you have exhausted every source of information available to you. All you have left is to go and talk to his friends, to his close friends, the people in whom he would confide."

"You want me to go and talk to Ismael Mario Zamora García."

"Yes, Alex. It seems to me you have no alternative. You need to go and talk to the top brass, as you call them, of the Sinaloa Cartel."

I sighed. "Yeah," I told him, "General Mike Ustinov is already seeing to the arrangements."

SEVEN

THE WOMAN PARKED ON THE STEEP, NARROW HILL
outside a one-story house that had been painted pastel blue.
It wasn't a great color for a house, but the one next to it on
the right was pastel pink, and the one of the left was terracotta, and the one next to that was yellow. It brought a kind
of joyous naivety to the street.

She climbed down from her Range Rover and pulled on
a broad-brimmed straw hat with a floral chiffon scarf tied
around the crown. In her khaki Bermuda shorts and her
brightly colored shirt, she was the living, breathing incarna-
tion of a different kind of naivety, the naivety which belongs
by antonomasia to the prosperous, liberal American middle
classes.

From the passenger seat descended a man in leather
sandals, khaki Bermuda shorts with too many pockets, a
shirt with too many parrots, a baseball cap and a big camera
around his neck.

The woman pointed down the road and said, "That's

it!" She squealed and added, "I am so *excited!* She said they were the best burritos she had *ever* eaten! *Ever!*" They headed down the hill together toward the Bar Don Felipe, in the village of Pericos. The woman kept talking. "And you know, honey, that Maria knows about burritos. I mean her mother is Mexican, right? And she knows a good burrito when she sees one."

"Right."

"And when she says—" She cut herself short as she pushed through the door. The place was empty, as you would expect at twelve o'clock. There would be no one there for at least an hour yet. She stopped, with her partner just behind her looking embarrassed, holding the door open and gaping. "Oh-my-*god!* I *love* it! Hank? Don't you love it? Isn't it just *perfect?*"

She caught sight of the guy behind the bar, leaning on his elbows and watching her from dark eyes. She pointed at him.

"Are you...um...*es usted don Miguelito*?"

He nodded a few times without smiling, watching her. She hurried across the floor, among the tables, in her rubber flip-flops, holding out both hands to him.

"You are *famous! Usted es famoso!*"

He didn't like that much and his frown came close to a scowl.

"Famous?" he said, in heavily accented English.

"You have the best burritos in the world! Wait!" She held up her hand, her fingers rigid and her nails very red. "I'm gonna say this in Spanish. *Usted los mejores burritos del mundo!* Um, um... In California, *todo el mundo*—everybody! *Everybody!*—*hablar* Miguelito's burritos! *Fantástico!*"

A cautious smile crawled across his face, like he wasn't sure whether to sell her a couple of burritos or cut her throat.

"I am espick English," he told her. "Better I espick English. You want burritos now?"

"Oh *yes!*" She put her hands together like she was praying and bobbed at the knees. "Oh, Hank! He's going to make us burritos! I am so excited!"

Hank rolled his eyes at Miguelito and said, "And two cold beers, please."

Miguelito nodded and jerked his chin at the tables. "You sit. I bring it to you."

Hank moved to the table, set down his camera and sat, but the woman hunched up like she was freezing in the snow and said, "I gotta go to the can, honey. I'll be right back. Don't start without me!" and she ran, in her strange, hunched position, to the toilets. Miguelito brought over the beers and set them on the table.

"You American?"

Hank nodded. "Yeah, from California."

Miguelito gave his head a small shake. "No many Americans comin' to this part of Mexico. They go to Mexico City, to Acapulco, Merida, Playa del Carmen..."

Hank did not miss the implied question. He nodded and smiled. "Yeah, I know, right? But me and Felicia, we don't believe everything we read in the papers, or we hear on TV. We wanted to see Mexico, right? But we wanted to see *real* Mexico, where the tourists don't go. So we have been to Sonora, we have been to Chihuahua, we have been to the Mapimi Biosphere Park, and let me tell you that place is extraordinary."

Miguelito grunted. "You gotta be careful, amigo. Sinaloa is a dangerous place. People real suspicious here. We see an American here and we think he is DEA. He can become dead real quick."

Hank gave a shrill laugh. "Oh, my goodness! DEA, no, we are certainly *not* DEA."

Miguelito smiled on one side of his face, where it was mildly offensive. "Yeah, I know. You know how I know?"

"No," following the phonetic flow.

Miguelito tapped his nose with a fat finger. "I can smell the DEA." He shook his head and grinned. "You no smell like DEA."

The toilet door opened behind them and Felicia trotted out making soft whooping noises. "Are those burritos ready? I cannot *wait!*"

Miguelito ignored her and walked away toward the bar and the kitchen. Felicia sat at the table and sipped her beer. "So, where is next on our itinerary, honey?"

Hank shrugged and made a little dance with his head. "I was thinking, you know, I wouldn't mind a good hotel, a pool and some margaritas. We could go to Merida, or Acapulco—"

"Oh those are boring places. That's where everybody goes."

"Yeah, I know hon, but Señor Miguel was telling me, it is pretty dangerous around here."

"That's stereotyping, Hank. I'm surprised at you!"

"Well, it's not stereotyping when it comes from Señor Miguel, who is a local, is it? I mean, it's not that they are going to rob us or kidnap us, honey. It's because they suspect Americans of being from the Drugs Enforcement Agency."

"Oh—my—god! Seriously? Nobody... I mean *nobody* could mistake *us* for federal agents, surely!"

Hunk pulled off half his beer while Felicia gaped at him, waiting for an answer. As he set down his glass he said, "Well that's what Señor Miguel said, he said he knew I wasn't because he could smell them. But," he gave a small laugh, "maybe not everyone has such a keen sense of smell, right? I think we have our burritos and then maybe move on to Merida or Acapulco for some luxury in the sun."

She pouted. "Oh, *Hank!*" She leaned across the table clutching her hands in an attitude of prayer, blowing kisses at him and saying, "Please, pretty please—"

Her elbow hit his camera and knocked it to the floor. She squealed and jumped up and immediately hunkered down to grab the camera, knocking over her chair in the process. Hank stood, exasperated, "Oh, *Felicia!*" and almost fell over her attempting to grab the chair. She squealed again and Hank squatted down, muttering, "Oh, here, give me that!" while she fell on her ass and scrambled up, picking up the chair in the process.

Miguelito emerged from the kitchen looking bored with a couple of burritos which he brought over to the table. As he set them down he asked, "You want more beer?"

Felicia laughed. "I think we need it!"

As he retreated to the bar to get the beers, Hank called after him, "Señor Miguel, I was telling my wife you recommend Acapulco, Merida and Playa del Carmen as places to go and visit, right?"

He watched them over the bar without expression and without answering. When he brought their drinks over and set them one by one on the table, he said, "If you are a

Yankee in Sinaloa, you don't want people to notice you." He directed his gaze at Felicia. "And everybody notice you, *señora*. You makin' a big mistake if you thinkin' Sinaloa is no dangerous. Sinaloa is very dangerous for you. I think is no good idea you go to Merida, or Acapulco or Playa del Carmen. My advices to you is, eat your burritos, drink your beers, get in your car and go directly to Mexicali or Tijuana, and back to California. At one o'clock my costomer beginnin' to come. You should go before they are arrivin'"

Hank was nodding. "I think that is good advice, honey. In fact, let me pay you now and we'll take the burritos to go."

They stood and Felicia collected up the burritos while Hank paid, and they both hurried out and back up the colorful hill to the Range Rover.

Miguelito returned to the bar, chuckling to himself. He knew they were harmless, but you didn't need to be DEA to get shot in Sinaloa. Americans were not popular, but the worst were the ones who practically pissed in their panties trying to show you they had nothing against Mexicans, that they didn't consider you inferior. When he was younger he would have raped her and made the pendejo Hank watch, then he would have cut Hank's throat and given the bitch to Ismael as a present. Now he was fifty. He had seen enough violence and pain—and fear. He had probably done them a favor. He knew Ismael was coming in today with his boys. If he had found those two here, he would have had a party with them. A party ending in a bloodbath.

He heard the door open and he looked up from washing the glasses. He smiled. This was one American he had no problem with. "Ian, *amigo mío!* What you doin', *cabrón?*"

He came round the bar as the colonel approached and they embraced. Then he held the colonel at arm's length and studied him. "You lookin' good! I heard you makin' a lot of money tellin' filthy lies about Sinaloa!"

They both laughed and the colonel climbed on a stool at the bar.

"I have been dreaming about Miguelito's beer, amigo. Give me a cold one."

"What you doin' here. I heard you was in New York, or London or some shit."

"I got tired of the rain, man. I needed some sunshine, some beautiful *señoritas*, see my old friends. Ismael is coming over, right? I said I'd meet him here at twelve thirty."

"Yeah, yeah." He nodded a few times. "He is comin' with Paco and some of the guys, you know Paco Gallardo, the one they call 'El Mecánico.'"

"Yeah, I know Paco. Me and Paco go way back."

They chatted for five minutes, remembering old times. Then the colonel said, "Hey, you know what I would love right now?"

Miguelito laughed. "Yeah, what everybody want. Burritos!"

"You got it, man!"

"OK, sit. I bring them over. Ismael gonna be here in a minute. I make enough for everybody."

He carried his beer over to the table where Hank and Felicia had been sitting a few minutes before. It was a round table and he chose the chair which was opposite Hank and Felicia's chairs, so that he was at six o'clock to their eleven and one. He took a pull of his beer and watched a large black Land Rover pull up outside. Behind it was a Jeep. The doors opened as men spilled out and closed like a volley of gunshots. Then the bar door opened and his old friend came in. But it was not Ismael Zamora, it was his right-hand man, Paco Gallardo, *el Mecánico*, followed by four men. A couple of them were well dressed and well groomed, and the colonel recognized them as nephews of Ismael's. The other four were muscle, Indians with aquiline features, dark skin and tattoos.

There was El Cuervo, with a jet-black ponytail down to his ass and a scar on his cheek that twisted his mouth into an ugly grin. There was El Sicaria, a skinny bastard with a crew cut and a bad speed habit, who liked to play with knives. Then there was El Abuelo, fat with a big moustache. He'd been around a long time and managed to survive, so they figured he was wise and they all trusted him. Even Ismael trusted him. The fourth guy was young and clean, the colonel didn't know him. He was new, and looked eager to prove himself.

The colonel grinned, but remained seated until the five men had approached the table. Then he stood and embraced Paco, *El Mecánico*.

"Come here, you son of a gun! I have missed you, man!"

They both laughed like he'd said something funny and Paco held him at arm's length. "You look good, *hijo de puta!* I been hearin' crazy things about you. You gonna bring down the US government single-handed, huh!"

The colonel laughed, slapped Paco on the shoulder and gestured at the chair where Felicia had been sitting. "C'mon, sit down. Miguel is making some burritos." He turned, grabbing the back of his chair for support, and hollered, "Hey, Miguelito! How about some beers here! *Traiga seis cervezas!*"

Miguel appeared behind the bar from the kitchen and nodded to *El Mecánico*.

"*Buenas tardes, patrón.*"

El Mecánico sat and his boys started dragging up chairs. Miguelito jerked his chin at the colonel. "I am always tellin' them. Don't try to espick Espanish. For God's sake, nobody understand you. Let me espick English. Is better."

They all roared with laughter. Miguelito loaded a tray with six jars of beer and carried them to the table. He set down *El Mecánico's* first, out of respect for the cartel. As the jug touched the table there was a loud *crack!* Like snapping wood, but as loud as a gunshot. *El Mecánico* gave a funny jump, his face collapsed like he was going to start crying like a child and a terrible wail escaped his mouth as fire and smoke began to billow from under his chair. Everybody stood, instinctively backing away from him. Chairs fell over. *El Mecánico* staggered to his feet and blood and gore spilled from between his legs. He wailed again and collapsed across the table.

There was a second of uncomprehending silence. Then a violent explosion, flat and agonizing on the ears, rocked the small bar. The door of the ladies' toilet was torn off its hinges and smoke and dust billowed into the room. Two more detonations, this time from flash-bangs, smashed the windows and brought the occupants to their knees, coughing and retching.

The colonel had known it was coming and had covered his ears. Now he watched as two silhouettes entered the bar through the billowing dust and smoke. He could see they were wearing gas masks and their assault rifles were fitted with laser sights. They were efficient and methodical, they double-tapped six times, twelve shots. Then they grabbed him by his arms and dragged him from the bar out into the street. They bundled him into the back of the Range Rover and drove away, not too fast and not too slow.

When they reached the Culliavan-Los Mochis Road they picked up speed and burned rubber until they came to Rancho Viejo. Just outside the town there was a woodland. Here they pulled off and followed a track in among the trees until they came to an old Ford Ranger XLT with the double cab. Here they dumped the Range Rover and transferred to the Ford, which they drove at a sedate pace south toward Zapotillo and then east, back toward Culiacan.

On the way the woman turned to the colonel who was sitting with his eyes closed in the back seat.

"Why didn't Zamora go?"

"You didn't give me time to ask." He paused a moment, watching her, then asked her, "What the hell did you do? It was disgusting. I never saw anything like it."

She glanced at the driver and smiled. "You want to tell him, Hank?"

"I'd love to, Felicia." They both laughed and he glanced in the mirror. "She stuck a one ounce C4 directional charge under his chair. That's why it was important you didn't sit there. It blew right up through the seat of the chair and basically cored him out."

The woman added, "The rest of it was a pound of C4 in the toilet and a couple of stun grenades. I told you there'd be fireworks."

"Yeah, you told me. Did you have to kill Miguelito?"

She turned and stared at him and there was real anger in her eyes. "You think he'll be missed because he was such a nice guy? You think the Sinaloa clan will miss his party tricks? The one where he snorts coke while he rapes a fifteen-year-old village girl? Or the one where he—"

"OK! OK! Spare me the sermon. You got what you wanted. Now what?"

"I didn't get what I wanted. I wanted Zamora. I didn't get him. So we go back and we try again, and again, and again, until I get him."

EIGHT

Mexico City is one of my least favorite cities. It's attractive, it has broad avenues and some beautiful buildings, and plenty of gardens, parks and leafy squares. And Mexicans, if one can generalize, are some of the nicest, friendliest people you could care to meet. It's a truism, and, like all truisms, it's true, that the violent minority that compose the cartels have given a beautiful people an ugly name. These are of course all reasons to like the city.

But there is something about a city that has names like the Angel of Independence Circus, Insurgents Avenue, Liberty Street, Workers' Colony and Park of the Illustrious Reporters that always makes me feel nervous, like the tanks are on permanent standby to roll onto Constitution Square. And in a country where the Attorney General reports that over twenty percent of the Federal Investigation Agency's operatives are suspected of working for the cartels, I guess you have to wonder just who would be sending out those tanks.

Still, the taxi ride from the airport, down Reform Avenue, was pleasant enough and at shortly before midday I climbed out of the cab into the sunshine, checked in at the Sheraton, dropped my bag in my room and took a stroll to the United States Embassy next door.

My Pentagon ID got me through security and I took the elevator to the fourth floor. A passage with a blue carpet and anonymous doors took me to the office of the CIA attaché, where his smiling secretary buzzed and told him, "Mr. Mason is here for you, Mr. Ortega."

He opened the door himself, grinning.

"Alex! How long's it been, dude?" He gripped my hand, slapped my shoulder and guided me into his office. "Five years? More? I couldn't believe it when I heard you were coming over. Siddown! You want a coffee, something stronger?"

The office was functional, with a window overlooking the inner yard. I sat in a blue, functional chair and he sat opposite me, behind his desk.

I shook my head. "No coffee, thanks, Bill, I'm fine. Listen, I'd love to catch up, but this is a flying visit and I need to get back as soon as possible. The office told you what it was about?"

He frowned and leaned back. "Superficially, but I can't pretend I understand. You want to talk to Zamora?"

"Yeah, I need to open a channel of communication with him and the Sinaloa top brass." I smiled. "I know you guys talk to them, it's an open secret and besides," I spread my hands, "I'm investigating the disappearance of Colonel Ian Cameron..."

The smile didn't exactly fade from his face, but it became a little strained.

"Right, sure, you know these things are very much compartmentalized..."

He let the words trail off because he knew as well as I did how stupid it sounded. I gave it a second and keeping the smile firmly in place, I said, "Right, and they have you as the Mexican attaché because this isn't your compartment?" He gave something between a cough and a laugh and I pressed him. "Come on, Bill, let's cut the bullshit. We're all on the same team here. I am not interested in what the Company gets up to in Mexico. I just need to talk to Zamora about Cameron."

"That's all?" The irony was palpable in the question. "The CIA's relationship with Sinaloa is a very sensitive subject, Alex. The director called me when your department approached him. I'll be straight with you. He told me to cooperate as far as I could without jeopardizing our operations here, but left it to my discretion to decide exactly what that entailed."

I watched him across the desk. He watched me back, waiting. Obviously he thought he'd said something that needed answering. I sighed.

"Bill, let me explain as simply as I can. Colonel Cameron has been abducted. Our analysis of the available intelligence throws up zero likely perps. We cannot find a single person or organization who would want to do this, but we also discount a publicity stunt. So we want to know—we *need* to know—who done it. Make sense so far?"

"Keep going."

"The colonel's friends are the Sinaloa top brass. He made those friends while he was working for you. So I can see why this is a sensitive matter for you. But we are not interested in that aspect of the case. We know you haven't got him. What's more," I shrugged, "if the Company is guilty of wrongdoing where Cameron and the Sinaloa are concerned, it's going to come out in his book in the next few days. So that's between you and the attorney general. We don't care. All we are interested in is finding out who took him, and why. We think Zamora and his pals might know. I talk to them, and then I go away."

"I need an undertaking from you, personally, that any information you might come across regarding the CIA's relationship with the Sinaloa Cartel will be kept confidential."

"You got it."

He opened a drawer and pulled out a document which he slid across the desk with a pen. "I am obliged to inform you that this is covered by title eighteen, of the US Code subsection seven ninety-eight. Do you understand that?"

"Yes, Bill, I understand that. Now can we cut the bullshit and do this. I haven't got a lot of time."

"Go back to your hotel. I have to make a couple of calls. I'll collect you in about an hour."

I nodded. "I appreciate it."

I walked the hundred yards back to my hotel, had a shower and changed my clothes, and just about had time for a burger and a beer before reception called to say that Mr. Guillermo Ortega was waiting for me in the lobby.

When I got down he was leaning on the reception desk, looking out through the plate-glass doors where there was a dark Dodge SUV parked, waiting. He saw me approaching from the elevators and came to meet me, slapped me on the shoulder and said, "Let's go for a ride."

As he guided me toward the door I asked him, "Mind telling me where?"

"Sure." We stepped out into the sunshine and a guy in a suit with dark shades and a wire in his ear opened the rear passenger door for me. I climbed in and Bill got in the other side. As he settled in his seat he said, "We're going to the St. Regis, big tower hotel five hundred yards down the road."

We pulled out into the honking, stop-start confusion of the Mexico traffic and turned right. I asked, "What's at the St. Regis?"

He smiled at me. "A heliport, on the roof. If we step on it we can be in Mazatlán in just over a couple of hours."

"Mazatlán? That's Sinaloa."

"Yeah, Ismael Zamora has agreed to meet us at his villa there."

"Us..."

"You and me. I'm coming with you, pal. Sinaloa and the Agency have a toxic, co-dependent relationship. We like to think we have the upper hand, and they like to think that *they* have the upper hand. The truth is, without Sinaloa we would be screwed in Latin America, for various reasons." He shrugged. "But equally, without the support of the CIA, Sinaloa wouldn't last a year."

I remembered something Nero had said once, which I had not understood at the time. He'd said, "There are few things the Pentagon fears more than a peaceful, prosperous Mexico." I frowned at Bill. "So while the White House arms and funds the Mexican government and military, you help Sinaloa...?"

He shrugged again. "Divide and conquer, Alex. Do you have any idea how rich and powerful Mexico could become if they got their shit together? We don't need that kind of competition in our backyard. This way is better, believe me."

He looked at me and laughed.

"What, you thought we stopped doing that kind of thing after Kennedy?"

"I guess not."

"Pal, great empires are not built on goodwill. Nobody wants to be colonized and exploited, except maybe the Europeans. And in this world, it is either colonize or be colonized. Sweden tried, and Switzerland, but they ended up being swallowed up by Brussels."

He looked out the window at the looming shape of the St. Regis Tower as we approached. He spoke absently. "Once you're in, you know, you can be nice." He glanced at me. "Build hospitals, compulsory education, roads and railways...but first you gotta get in. OK, we're here."

We pulled in to the shade of the covered entrance and Bill was already climbing out. I got out after him and followed him through the big brass and plate-glass doors into the vaulted lobby. We made our way across the gleaming marble floor to the bank of elevators and he called the one on the far right. It pinged, the doors slid open and when we climbed in he held a plastic card over a sensor above the keypad and the doors closed and we started to climb silently. We passed the penthouse suites and slowed to a halt. The doors hissed and clunked open. We stepped out into a passage with an emergency stairwell on the right, and a steel door forty or fifty feet on our right. On our left was another steel door that led to the elevator winch room. It had a picture of a guy being struck down by a lightning bolt on it.

Bill led the way to the steel door, opened it with his fob and we stepped out onto a large, blue-gray roof with a big, white H on it. I watched him scan the sky a moment, then he pointed and grinned at me. "There she comes!"

I looked where he was pointing, across the rooftops of Mexico City far below. There was a small, black speck approaching from the direction of the airport. I looked back at his face and asked him the question that had been on my mind since we'd got in the car.

"Whose side are you on, Bill?"

He frowned at me, but I didn't wait for an answer. I pulled out my cell and called Odin. When Lovelock came on the line I said, "Put me through to Nero. I'm in kind of a hurry. I've got a chopper coming and I want him to hear me before it starts beating the air around here."

Bill was scowling. A moment later Nero came on the line. "Well?"

"Sir, I am at the St. Regis Tower helipad. I am about to get on a chopper with Bill—that's Guillermo Ortega, the CIA's attaché at the Mexican embassy. We're on our way to Mazatlan, in Sinaloa, to meet with Ismael Zamora. He has a villa outside town."

"Good. You are telling me this why?"

I didn't answer for a moment. I looked Bill in the eye and said, "I'm not sure. Maybe because the Agency and Sinaloa have a toxic, co-dependent relationship."

"I see. I shall be aware of it. When should I expect to hear from you?"

"Tonight, before midnight."

"Good, I am sure Mr. Ortega is aware of ODIN's reach."

I put it on speaker and said, "I'm sorry, sir, could you repeat that?"

"I say that I am quite sure Mr. Ortega is aware of ODIN's reach."

I smiled at Bill. "I am sure he is, sir."

I hung up. We could hear the chopper approaching. Bill shook his head and raised his voice. "You didn't need to do that."

I patted his shoulder. "That's the thing with toxic relationships, Bill. You never know what you need to do and what you don't need to do. And you end up doing crazy things you didn't really want to do at all."

The chopper landed in a hail of noise and downdraft, and we ran, hunched against the blades of the rotors, and clambered into the cabin behind the pilot. We strapped ourselves in and I hauled the door shut. Bill called, *"OK, let's go!"* and a moment later we were rising high above the city, banking slightly and hurtling north and west toward the Pacific coast.

Bill was quiet for a long while, till all we could see beneath us was the peaks of the Sierra Madre, as we moved steadily toward Michoacán and Guanajauto. Then he turned to me frowning and said, "Look, Alex, what I said. I never meant you to take it the way you did."

"I know that."

"I was talking about the Agency as a whole, as an institution, not me, personally."

I held his eye a moment. "Can you make that distinction, Bill? How long have you been with the CIA, twenty years?"

"Twenty-two."

"Can you really separate yourself from them that clearly? Can you look me in the eye and tell me the CIA's relationship with Sinaloa isn't the same as your relationship with Ismael Zamora?"

He screwed up his face and turned away to look out the window. After a moment he looked back at me and there was resentment in his eyes.

"Of course I can, Alex. You ain't gonna go taking tales back to DC, are you? You could destroy me. I got a wife and kids..."

"Relax, will you? I'm not carrying tales to anybody. Besides," I smiled, making him a part of the joke, "since when does ODIN give information to the Company? We might screw it out of you, but we never share."

He managed half a grin. "Yeah, that's true enough."

"Relax, Bill. I'm just being cautious and covering my back. You'd do the same."

He nodded and we flew on in silence.

An hour later, or a little more, the mountains began to fall away beneath us and the vast, gleaming sheet of the Pacific appeared in the distance, ahead and to our left. Pretty soon the pilot pointed and called back to us, "*Mazatlán!*"

I leaned over to look and saw the urban sprawl on the edge of the ocean. From north, south and east roads converged on the town. I realized we seemed to be following one of those roads, and banking east of the town. Five minutes later we were descending, flying low, first over fields of crops, and then over forested peaks, with the treetops hurtling past a couple of hundred feet below us. And then we could see it, in a clearing in the forest, a vast, sprawling ranch, with very white walls and corrugated, terracotta roofs. At a glance I saw what seemed to be stables and garages at the back of the main building. There was a pool and a couple of tennis courts. A large lawn spread out in front of the houses, and we slowed, hovered and gently landed.

I climbed out under the idling rotors, with Bill just behind me, and saw maybe seventy or eighty yards away, a group of half a dozen men trotting down the steps from the porch outside the front door. Four of them were dressed in jeans and casual shirts or T-shirts. One wore a pale gray business suit, and the other wore a gleaming white double-breasted suit with shiny black shoes. I turned to Bill and shouted above the thud of the rotors.

"Do I get points for guessing which one is Zamora?"

He smiled and shook his head. "Nope, we both get points for getting out of here alive." He held my eye a moment. "You may not believe me, pal, but I am laying my life on the line bringing you here."

I studied his face a second, wondering if he was lying. "That toxic, huh?"

He nodded. "Yeah," and he turned to watch the approaching men. "Sometimes that toxic."

NINE

WE DUCKED OUT FROM UNDER THE DOWNDRAFT and went to meet the approaching men. They stopped and fanned out and we stopped eight or ten feet away from them as the turbine whined and died behind us.

The man in the white suit, whom I had assumed was Ismael Zamora, narrowed his eyes and examined me minutely. He had thick, blue-black hair slicked back. Fine features that were more Indian than Spanish, and a clean-shaven jaw and upper lip. He was younger-looking than I had expected, maybe in his early forties. Then he turned and looked at Bill.

"I am not happy, Bill. You make me miss a reunion with friends. What is it for? To meet this gringo?"

Bill spread his hands. "I'm sorry about that, Ismael. You scratch my back today, you know I'll scratch yours when you need it." He glanced at me and added, "Within reason. This is important or we wouldn't do it. You know that."

He turned to me. "OK, so what do you want?"

I arched my eyebrows like I was mildly surprised. "You mean other than a chair to sit in, a drink and some courtesy?"

He snorted, gave me the once-over and then did one of those elaborate complicated gestures where you shrug, make a face, spread your arms and make a smaller second shrug-within-a-shrug that only Latin peoples know how to do. It is the body language equivalent of "Sure, what the hell do I know, go ahead, I don't care." Then he jerked his head toward his veranda and we all headed that way.

The guys in jeans stood. Bill, the guy in the gray suit, Zamora and I sat on cane chairs and a girl in a French maid's uniform was dispatched to get drinks. While she was getting them Zamora lit a cigarette and waved it in my direction with a stream of smoke wafting from his mouth as he spoke.

"OK, Gringo, now you got your chair, your drink and your courtesy. What do you want? I suppose to be one hundred fifty miles from here, havin' a party."

"My name is Alex Mason. And I'll make a deal with you. You don't call me Gringo and I won't call you Narco." There was an intense stillness at the table, and for a moment I wished I still smoked, because that would have been the moment to take my time lighting up a Camel. Instead, I held his eye for a count of four and went on.

"I understand you and Colonel Ian Cameron are close friends."

His eyes shifted to Bill. There was a small shrug and a narrowing of his eyes. "*Que es esto?*"

He was asking him what the hell was going on. I didn't give Bill time to answer.

"Mr. Zamora, there is not much point in your asking

Bill that question because he doesn't know the answer. In fact, at this point I am going to ask if you and I can speak privately, because I did not expect Bill to accompany me." I turned to Bill who was scowling at me again and told him, "Sorry Bill, this is highly classified and I am not authorized to share it with you."

Zamora was frowning hard by now. After a moment he nodded to the gray suit and jerked his head at Bill. Bill babbled, "Yeah, sure, no problem. I get it. No sweat," and he and the gray suit went inside. The girls brought out a tray with an unopened bottle of Bushmills and a couple of crystal tumblers. He offered it to me to inspect, then opened it and poured two glasses.

"What do you want with Colonel Cameron? I ain't seen him in a long time."

"Mr. Zamora, you know very well, from your own personal experience," I spread my hands, "from your contact with Colonel Cameron himself, that the CIA is a law unto itself, and whatever they do, the administration that is in power tends to turn a blind eye."

He shrugged. "Maybe. So?"

"So not every department of the intelligence community operates in the same way. I represent a different department, and we are concerned that the CIA may be attempting to assassinate the colonel."

His eyes were hooded and inscrutable. He waited.

"The fact is, Colonel Cameron was abducted in New York a couple of nights ago at the launch of his new book. You have heard about his book?"

He nodded slowly, but there was no change to his expression.

"His book is upsetting a lot of people. We don't know if it has upset them enough to want him dead, or how much good they think that will do, but the CIA has to be high on our list of suspects. However..."

"You think we took him?"

"No. Why would you? His book is a coup for you. But like I say, if the colonel shows up dead, it is just going to corroborate everything he says in his book. So that is not going to help any of the people or the organizations he names. So..."

"You are thinkin'," he smiled, "maybe his pals in Sinaloa know something you don't."

"That's about the size of it, Mr. Zamora."

"Why do you care. He's a problem. When he's dead, pretty soon he stops bein' a problem. We say, *muerto el perro, se acabo la rabia*. When the dog is dead, the rabies is finished."

"Well, that's true up to a point. But when the problem is people thinking they are free to go around kidnapping and killing people, then with every dog that dies, you actually have more rabies. Kidnapping and murdering people, even people like Colonel Ian Cameron, is against the law. And it should be against the law, Mr. Zamora. So if somebody kidnaps a person on 5th Avenue, then we need to find that kidnapper and punish them. It's called civilization."

He threw his head back and laughed out loud. "You think America is a civilized, law-abiding country? You're outta your mind!"

"I am not here to sell you an image of the United States, Mr. Zamora. You asked me why I care and I told you. I'll say this, though. If a society, any society, mine, yours, Denmark,

Canada, wherever, is slowly disintegrating into chaos and anarchy, does it help if we all just shrug and say, 'Ah, hell, I'm going to kill my neighbor and steal his TV. And if the cops show up I'll kill them too!' Would that help to stop the chaos and the anarchy? But if enough people take responsibility..."

I trailed off. He said, "You better stop, I think I am gonna be sick. I feel like I fell through the lookin' glass into *Little House on the Prairie*. So you wanna know who I think abducted the colonel." He stared out at the trees. "I gotta tell you," he said at last, and shook his head. "I gotta tell you. I don't know if somebody is tryin' to play me here."

"Play you how?"

"OK, so maybe the *hijos de puta* of the Gulf Cartel? They got plenty of reason to wanna kill Ian. He hurt them bad. He helped us to hurt them real bad. But now?" He narrowed his eyes at me and hunched his shoulders. "Why now? He's been livin' quiet in London and in New York. They can't send a *sicario* over to London or New York and cut his throat? They gotta wait till he is launching his book and he is walkin' down 5th Avenue? That don't make no sense."

"I agree. So?"

Suddenly his face creased up and he laughed out loud again. "So it is one of two possibilities. One," he held up a finger, "you are trying to play me. But I can't see what play you think you gonna pull. And the other is that Ian is playin' you. You wanna know where I am supposed to be right now?"

I stared at him long and hard. Finally I said, "Meeting Colonel Ian Cameron."

"He call me last night. Paco went with some boys to meet him. I was gonna go but I gotta come here for this stupid meeting with you." He glanced at his watch. "We got no signal up here or I would call him so he can talk to you and we have a good laugh. Right now they are at my villa, drinkin', snorting coke, playin' with the girls in the pool." His eyes narrowed and there was something reptilian about his smile. "You and Bill are welcome. You can come along for the party. Maybe we can talk some business."

"Thanks, I'll pass."

I took my time sipping my whiskey, trying to assimilate and process what he had just told me. I couldn't because it didn't make any sense. I looked him in the eye and shook my head. "No—"

"No? You sayin' I am lying?"

"No. If the colonel really is a friend of yours, do him a favor and don't tell Bill about any of this. I don't know if Cameron is in Mexico, where he called you from or why, but I will tell you this. His abduction on 5th Avenue was not a stunt. And I will be very surprised if when you get back to your villa Colonel Ian Cameron is there. I won't waste any more of your time. I'm going to let you get back to your party. But do me a favor, will you?"

"What favor?"

"If the colonel is there, get him to call me." I handed him a card. "That is my private number. And if he's not, you call me and tell me what happened."

He took the card and examined it, then raised his eyes to meet mine.

"You think the CIA want to silence him? Maybe I should keep Bill here."

"No, I told you. The CIA doesn't make sense. Neither do any of the other people he names in his book. That's why I am here, Mr. Zamora. To see if you, his friend and his ally, know who might be doing this. You are the only person I can think of who might have that kind of information."

He shook his head. "No, I don't know. I'm gonna keep Bill here. If something has happened to Ian, I will send his head to Langley in a box."

"I wouldn't recommend that, Mr. Zamora. You do that and I will personally ensure that every one of your villas and farms is razed to the ground, and I'll have you hung from your ankles until your brain explodes." I leant forward and looked into his eyes. "We are not the CIA, Mr. Zamora. We don't play games, we don't get in the news, and we don't make mistakes. Fuck with me, and I will eat your heart for breakfast."

I stood and walked to the door like I was really sure he was not going to shoot me in the back. I leaned on the jamb and saw Bill inside sitting on the sofa, staring at a glass of whiskey in his hands. He looked up.

"You done?"

"Yeah, let's go."

As we crossed the veranda back toward the lawns, Zamora didn't get up. He watched us and when we got to the steps he said, "Mason." I stopped to look at him. "I'm gonna call you in a couple of hours, when I get back to my villa. But don't you ever fockin' threaten me again."

I gave a nod that didn't mean much. "Nobody gets something for nothing, Zamora. Cooperation gets you cooperation, threats get you threats. You've got to be smart enough to assess how powerful your enemy is before you start threatening him or his friends."

It was a long walk across the lawn back toward the chopper. When we had climbed in and slammed the door, they stood on the veranda watching us while the rotors started their slow thud. They picked up speed and finally the chopper began to rock slightly and we were climbing, hovering, and gaining height. I looked down and saw Zamora, in his white suit, trot down the steps and stare up at us as we banked north and east and started our return journey, back toward Mexico City.

After a while Bill looked at me and his face was twisted with resentment.

"You put my life on the line back there."

"Not me, Bill, the Agency."

"What?"

"I asked you to arrange a meeting. I didn't ask you to come along and hold my hand. The Agency told you to do that because they want to know what I'm doing and what I know about the colonel and his whereabouts." I gave a small shrug. "You were sent to spy on me."

"Excluding me from the meeting like that," he shook his head, "I have lost face with Zamora now, I have lost their respect, and worse than that you have given them the idea that the Agency might be responsible for Cameron's abduction."

"Yes, and my advice to you is, when you get back to the office, tell your boss to keep his damned nose out of ODIN's business in future. If you want something, ask. If we can give it to you we will."

We were quiet for a while, moving steadily over the

mountains, with the afternoon sun reflecting off the Pacific Ocean on our starboard side.

"If you're lucky," I told him, "Cameron will be at Zamora's villa when he gets back home."

He frowned at me. "What are you talking about?"

I smiled. "I wish I knew, Bill." I saw no reason not to tell him. "According to Zamora, Cameron called him last night and they arranged to meet today, at Zamora's place, for a party."

"So it *is* all a stunt."

"It looks that way."

Something in my voice made him squint and then throw up his hands.

"Same old Alex! They have a saying in Mexico, you know? *Buscándole cinco patas al gato.* You know what it means?"

"Enlighten me."

"You're always looking for the cat's fifth leg. He ain't got one. What more do you need? The guy is a scoundrel, always has been. That's why the Agency recruited him, for Christ's sake! Now he's blowing the whistle on everyone, and what is the best way to boost sales? Get 'abducted,'" he made little speech marks with his fingers, "go and spend a week or two snorting coke and getting laid by *señoritas* at Zamora's pad, and then return home to an international bestseller." He pointed a finger at me like a gun. "And he has another good reason for coming to hang out with his old pal. He is safe from reprisals from the Agency and from any of the other names he has named who might get it into their heads to punish him."

I nodded. "That all makes sense."

"So?"

"So the snatch was all wrong, Bill. It was discreet. When, in his entire life, has Colonel Ian Cameron been discreet? If he had planned this there would have been a whole show, gunfire, squealing tires, and maybe some boys from the press and footage for the news and YouTube."

He nodded, stared out at the gathering dusk and said, "I hear you, but you are overlooking something important." He looked back at me. "Cameron was nothing if not a very careful, methodical planner. Yeah, sure, he might have wanted the big Hollywood style kidnapping where he comes off as an all-American rogue hero. But he would have thought it through and decided that, if he made a whole show of it, the risk of getting caught by the cops was too great. Do it on Lafayette in the Bronx and maybe you get away with it. But on 5th Avenue and 59th, outside the Plaza? That's a big risk. Plus," he gave his head another quick shake, "he didn't know he was going to have Alex Mason on his case analyzing every minute detail and looking for five legs on the cat."

It made sense. I sighed. "We'll see what Zamora says when he gets home."

"He should get there about the same time as we get back to the hotel." After a moment he frowned. "Hey, no hard feelings, right. It's the job."

I nodded. "Sure. It's the job."

When we arrived at Mexico City Bill offered to give me a ride to the hotel, but I decided to take the five or ten-minute walk along the *Paseo de la Reforma* and clear my head. I watched him climb into the back of the dark SUV, told him I'd be in touch, and watched him drive away into the evening traffic. Then I thrust my hands into my pockets and strolled east toward my hotel. I shoved the Chinese puzzle of the colonel's abduction into my unconscious with instructions to sort it out, and allowed my conscious mind to take in the attractive avenue, the Argentine restaurant, the bakers shop, the cinema and Brad's Beers, the terraced bar beside the Japanese restaurant. Suddenly a cold beer seemed like a good idea and I stepped up to a table intending to sit down.

Something about the small crowd at the bar inside made me pause. Peering through the reflections in the plate-glass wall, I could see they were staring at the TV behind the bar. I stepped inside and leaned on the doorjamb. The TV showed a steep, narrow street with a bar on the corner. You could just make out the name. Bar Don Felipe. There was smoke drifting from the door and the windows, not like a raging fire, more like something was smoldering inside.

The scene changed and there were images of inside the bar. The floor was littered with bodies. I counted seven. There were chairs turned over, but one in particular was charred and partially burned and had a body lying beside it with most of his lower body blown apart. The camera closed in and I recognized Francisco Gallardo, Zamora's right-hand man. I couldn't follow the narrative, but I heard the word Sinaloa repeated several times and stepped up to the bar. A guy I figured was Brad asked me, "What'll it be?"

"A cold beer." I jerked my head at the TV. "What happened?"

He put an iced jug under the tap. "Massacre in Pericos, just outside Culiacán. Seven members of the Sinaloa Cartel shot dead in one of their hangouts; including Francisco Gallardo, one of the top guys." He set the beer in front of me. "They had a special treat for him. They put an ounce of C4 under his chair. Talk about a pain in the ass, huh?"

I winced. "Any word on who did it?"

He shook his head. "Speculation. Maybe the Gulf, or one of the other smaller cartels. The way I see it, seven less bastards in the world. They should send in the army and wipe 'em out."

I nodded, paid for the beer and carried it outside. I had sat and taken my first pull when the phone rang. I wasn't surprised to find it was Zamora.

"Did you do this, *Gringo de mierda*?"

"You want to explain that to me, Zamora? Because, see, I am having some trouble following your logic. I get Cameron to arrange to meet you and your boys at the Bar Don Felipe, so that I can ambush and massacre you. And then at the last minute I arrange to meet you a hundred and fifty miles away from the ambush. For what? So I can ask you where Cameron is. I'm not seeing it."

"Ian would not do this! So who did it?"

"I'm guessing the colonel was not there."

"No. Nobody was there and there were no witnesses. Everybody dead, including Miguelito."

"So whoever abducted the colonel hit your men."

His voice was a rasp. "*But who?*"

"Well, that's what I was trying to ask you this afternoon, Zamora, before you decided it would be smart to abduct and murder the CIA's attaché at the American embassy."

"It must be the CIA!"

"Zamora, get your testicles out of your brain and try thinking, will you? Who called you to arrange a meeting with me?"

"Bill."

"Would Bill have done that if the CIA was arranging an ambush to wipe out the heads of the Sinaloa Cartel? Or would he have told me he'd called but you couldn't make it till next week?"

His voice came as a shrill scream, "*Then who, pendejo de mierda! Who done this to me?! I want them! I gonna take their skin and roll them in fockin salt!*"

"Zamora, I think you need to go sit in the naughty corner and think about the language you're using. When you have calmed down, you put your toys back in the pram and, if you have something useful to say, call me."

I hung up, finished my beer and strolled back to my hotel.

TEN

THE CAR CAME IN THE NIGHT, INTO THE SILENT
sleeping village square. This was on the borders of Sinaloa
territory, and the townspeople had long since learned the
wisdom of the three monkeys. So nobody saw the car arrive,
and if they heard it, they simply squeezed their eyes tight and
fled into their dreams.

It was a Land Rover Defender V8 in matte black, it had
its headlamps switched off and it rolled quietly to the hotel
in the dusty town square of Rosario. There it parked beside
the dusty old Ford pickup. And waited.

Two minutes later the door opened and the woman
came out with two of her boys. The doors of the Defender
opened and two men got out. They didn't speak. The five
went to the trunk of the Land Rover and opened it, and
between them they began to unload boxes, which they transferred to the pickup. But they didn't stash them in the cargo
bed. They stashed them on the rear seat and on the floor.

Then the two men got back in the Defender and drove away in silence.

The woman checked her watch. It was one AM. She and her two boys went back inside the hotel. The boys went to their room but she went to the room where the colonel was sleeping, cuffed to the bed. She had her bed made on the floor. There she lay down, with a Maxim 9 internally suppressed semi-automatic by her side, and instructed her unconscious mind to awaken her at three fifty-five, in two hours and fifty minutes. Then she systematically relaxed all her muscles and went into deep sleep.

Two hours and fifty minutes later she sat up, stood, slipped the Maxim in her waistband and shook the colonel awake. She un-cuffed him, made him stand and cuffed his hands behind his back. A moment later the man she called Dave came in with coffee. He put hers on the table while she splashed cold water on her face, and helped the colonel to drink his.

Five minutes later she was leading him down the stairs. The hotel was silent and sleeping, and their boots on the stairs sounded excessively loud. But no one stirred, no one peered out to see what was happening.

They stepped out into the darkness before dawn, where a couple of frail lamps cast lonely amber light on the cool dust of the square. She bundled him into the front passenger seat and swung in behind the wheel. The engine roared and they pulled out of the square and onto the 190 toward Fundición and the Via Mex-15 D.

By the time they got there the eastern horizon was turning a blue-gray, but dawn was still an hour away. The highway was empty when they rolled onto it and she put her foot down. On the outside the truck looked a wreck, but on the inside the boys had replaced just about everything from the suspension to the engine and the wiring. It had two hundred and fifty horses under the hood and could do a hundred and thirty miles an hour and corner at ninety without rolling over.

Not that that was going to be a problem. They were going to follow the Via Mex-15 for the next two hundred and fifty miles, and it was about as straight as a road could get without going to the Dakotas. She figured three hours would get her to Culiacán.

As they passed the desolation of Agiabampo in the early dawn, with its sparse lights and dusty roads among tumble-down shacks, the colonel spoke for the first time.

"Where are you taking me?"

"I told you yesterday."

"You did? I don't remember."

"We're going to get Zamora."

He laughed. "We're going to get Zamora? You and me? He probably has twenty men in his house, all armed with latest generation weapons provided by the CIA courtesy of the United States government. What are you going to do, walk in, show him your pretty ass and ask him to come for a picnic?"

She didn't answer. They drove on in silence.

As they crossed the border from Sonora into Sinaloa, the sun began to creep over the mountains in the east. The colonel spoke suddenly and his voice sounded loud in the cab.

"Who are you?" She smiled but said nothing. "Come on,

you're going to kill me anyway. What difference does it make if you tell me who's killing me?"

"What makes you think I'm going to kill you?"

His voice came laden with sarcasm. "Gosh, I don't know. It might have something to do with the fact that you have me handcuffed in a truck, and yesterday you massacred seven men in a bar in Pericos."

He waited, but she didn't answer. After a while he narrowed his eyes. "You look Mexican to me. Did your family get killed and you blame me for it?"

She glanced at him. "You think that's likely."

He made a face and shrugged. "Yeah, could be. Are you connected with the Gulf, Zeta...?"

"You are telling me that you are responsible for so many deaths, that there is a good probability that, if I am Mexican, my family was killed because of you."

"Hell! You put it like that...Jesus!"

"Shut up, Colonel. I mean it." She turned to look at him. "Seriously, shut up or I'll cut your damned tongue out."

At just after eight AM they passed the Culiacán Seminary on their right and, a mile down the road, they crossed the highway and took a broad dirt track that wound through small fields to the tiny village of Santa Maria. From there they ground on along an ever worse track, into the sierra of the *Cerro de la Chiva*, where the farmland fell away and was replaced by dense pinewoods.

Pretty soon they were jolting and lurching along a footpath with visibility among the trees down to twenty yards or less. And finally, at close to half-past nine, the track petered out in a small clearing. At the far end the trees thinned out where the land fell away toward a valley. The woman killed the engine and swung down from the cab. She walked around the hood, her boots crunching on the thick carpet of pine needles, and she wrenched open the passenger door and hauled the colonel out.

Taking his arm she dragged him across the clearing and, where the trees thinned out, she kicked him in the back of the knee and hurled him down on the ground. Then she hunkered down beside him and pointed across the valley below them.

"See that villa? Do you recognize it? About a mile away."

He struggled and writhed to pull himself into a sitting position, then looked.

"Yeah, you know I do. It's Zamora's place."

"Right."

Without explanation she undid his boots, removed the laces and tied his ankles together. The boots she carried back to the truck and threw them in back. Then she began to unload wrapped bundles and packages from the rear passenger seats. These she carried over to where the colonel was sitting and started to unpack them. The first was a telescope with a tripod. This she put together quickly and trained it on the villa. When it was set up she glanced at the colonel.

"You know what this is? Latest generation. It's equipped with an infrared laser that puts up a digital display at the bottom of the image and tells you exactly, to the inch, where your target is." She put her eye to the scope and smiled. "That is a nice house. Big pool, and there they all are, lounging, drinking margaritas. I count..." She paused, then, "fifteen guys including Zamora, and five women. Come here."

She grabbed him by the scruff of his neck and dragged him to his feet. "Tell me, which one is Zamora?"

He stared for a moment, then said, "He's the one in the dark blue Bermudas with the floral shirt and the black Wayfarers. He's sitting on the left of the pool, under the lime-green parasol."

"Good, go sit down."

He returned to the tree and slid down, watching her. "What are you, a sniper? That's a mile. You gonna take him out from a mile away?"

She didn't answer. She was unpacking several cartons and started assembling some kind of artifact made of pale blue hardened plastic. He watched as it began to take shape, and when she snapped the two motors into the engine mounts and fitted the four lithium batteries, he muttered, "Sweet Jesus, it's a drone."

She stood and looked down at it where it sat on the ground. It was five and a half foot long and four foot wide, sleek and eminently aerodynamic in design.

"Not exactly, Colonel. It has an onboard computer," she pointed at the telescope, "that is linked to the infrared laser. When I switch the controls to automatic, it accelerates to five hundred miles per hour in one point five seconds and the laser tells it exactly where to go."

She hunkered down and ripped open two more cartons. They contained two long boxes of hardened plastic, five foot long and maybe a foot wide. She opened these and, with difficulty, extracted two metal cylinders, which she slotted into the drone, one on either side. When she was done she turned to the colonel.

"There is fifty-five pounds of C4 in each of those canisters. One hundred and ten pounds total. The C4 is attached to a canister of compressed liquid, carbon-based gas with very fine aluminum particles in it. There will be an initial explosion which will do a lot of damage." She smiled. "A hundred and ten pounds of C4 makes a big bang, but the real damage comes when the vaporized gas expands into a cloud and is ignited by a second, small explosion. That aluminum burns hot." She paused a moment, holding the colonel's eye. "I guess it's appropriate. For Ismael Zamora, there is no escape from hell."

He said, "It's called a thermobaric bomb, and it is illegal."

"Yeah, like murder, heroin and cocaine."

She took the black plastic remote control unit and after a moment the powerful rotors began to spin, and the drone rose steadily up through the tall pines and began to climb toward the sky. Pretty soon its pale blue belly had vanished against the sky. Its electric motors, driven by the immensely powerful lithium batteries, were inaudible.

On the remote control unit the screen showed her what the drone's cameras were seeing. From a thousand feet she looked down and saw the house with clarity, the large pool on the spacious terrace. She peered through the telescope and confirmed Zamora's position and fixed the infrared targeting laser on his belly, then brought the drone around so that its trajectory and momentum, having struck Zamora, would carry the debris and the cloud of gas into the house.

She flipped the switch to automatic. There was a time-less moment of absolute silence.

The drone was a thousand feet up and half a mile from its target. In a heartbeat it had accelerated to its maximum speed and had covered half the distance. It was still invisible and completely inaudible above the laughter and the music of the party. Another second and Ismael Maria Zamora Garcia just had time to frown and squint at the strange shimmering in the air. Then two hundred and twenty pounds of explosive drone plunged into his belly and split him in half. His consciousness in this world lasted just long enough to tell him he felt very strange, and then he was atomized by a massive explosion which hurled his parasol like a molten javelin across the terrace, shattered the plate glass in doors and windows, vaporized the surface of the pool and tore the people closest to him literally limb from limb.

There was a fraction of a second of silence after the ghastly, flat bang of the initial detonation, and then the entire terrace and the house were engulfed in an infernal eruption of expanding, incinerating gas that set fire to everything in its path.

The few that survived the first explosion staggered, unable even to scream, danced diabolically and fell, charred and dehumanized.

Colonel Ian Cameron sat with his back against the pine and watched Zamora's home burn. The woman watched it through the telescope for thirty seconds. When she was satisfied, she collected up her equipment and piled it back in the Ford. When she returned for the colonel, while she was untying his ankles, he said, "That was not revenge."

She stood. "Get up."

He pushed himself to his feet, leaning his back against the tree.

"That," he said, "was a message."

"Get in the truck."

He picked his way, wincing, across the pine needles. She opened the passenger door for him and he climbed in. She slammed the door and got in behind the wheel.

"A message," he said again. "But, if you just killed the head of the cartel, who is the message for?"

She turned the truck around and started rolling back toward the road. The colonel was frowning harder, looking out at the green shade of the huge pines.

"And, another thing, what the hell did you need me here for?"

She glanced at him. "As a witness."

"A witness?"

The wheel jumped and lurched in her hands as she negotiated the pitted track.

"You're going to write a postscript to your book, an author's note."

"Saying what?"

"I'll let you know when the time comes."

"So what happens now?"

"Now we go to Canada."

He stared at her like she was crazy. "*Canada?*"

"Yeah, to Calgary, to visit your friend, General Mike Ustinov."

He sank back in his seat. "Holy shit!" He turned and stared at her. "You're on a mission. Who the hell are you?"

"You'll find out, Colonel. Believe me, you'll find out."

ELEVEN

I was dressing after a late breakfast of eggs and bacon in my room when my cell rang.

"Mason—"

"Are you watching the news?"

"Good morning, Bill. What am I supposed to be watching?"

"It's breaking now. Go to CNN. I am going to get off the line because you'll want to call your boss."

I switched on the TV and found CNN's breaking news. The view was from a chopper circling over a villa which was partially engulfed in flames, billowing smoke across a wide valley. You could just make out fire trucks trying to douse the flames. A voice was saying, "Facts are woefully thin on the ground. The Sinaloa Cartel is not talking, and the Mexican government seems to have been taken as much by surprise as the cartel has. One thing we do know is that this is one of a number of residences belonging to Ismael Mario Zamora Garcia, the notorious head of the Sinaloa Cartel.

"However, whether he was actually at the villa when it was struck is not clear. Some sources, who understandably wish to remain anonymous, say that Zamora had traveled south to Mazatlán, but others state categorically that he had returned in the same day and was at home, mourning the loss, just the day before, of his right-hand man, Francisco Gallardo."

They cut back to the studio. The anchor, frowning at the camera, asked, "Are we looking at an escalation of the conflict between—" But he was cut short and put his hand to his ear. "Pete, I am just hearing, this has just come through, several bodies have been recovered from the terrace at the villa, and one of the bodies, badly mutilated, has been identified as that of Ismael Mario Zamora Garcia."

"Yes, I am hearing the same thing. What is still not clear, though, is exactly how this strike was carried out. It seems to have been some kind of rocket, but…"

I switched off the TV and called Nero. It rang once and he said, "I am watching it now."

"This is not a stunt. This is punitive. Somebody is sending a message."

"I agree. But there is little point in sending messages to people you have just massacred. This message was not for Sinaloa."

"No, the message was for the US government and administration."

"They have not finished. The message is not complete. You know who is next."

"General Mike Ustinov. I need to get to Calgary, fast. We should pull him into protective custody. I don't want to call him. Aside from the fact that he's probably in the mountains hunting, he won't be cooperative. I need his address, and I need to know where his cabin is."

"Agreed. Go and get him."

"Sir, do you know who is doing this?"

"I have some ideas."

"Care to share."

"No. I must make some inquiries."

"I'll need the Valkyrie—"

The Valkyrie was what we had taken to calling ODIN's Gulfstream G 500, which had a range of over five thousand nautical miles and could remain airborne for up to ten hours solid.

"I assume this is some misnomer for the company jet. The mere fact that it flies does not make it a Valkyrie. Valkyrie collected those courageous warriors who were killed in battle and carried them to the Hall of the Fallen—that is what Val Halla means, Alex—the Fallen Hall. I assume you are in no hurry to arrive there just yet."

"Thank you sir, you are not only informative, but fun, too. Can I expect the Gulfstream G 500 aeromobile within the next few hours?"

"I take it you are being facetious, Alex. I shall alert the transport department and they will contact you with their arrival time at Mexico's International Airport. I should say you have a good five or six hours."

"I may need a suppressed weapon, too. Can you send me a Maxim 9 with the jet?"

"I'll see to it."

"I'll keep you posted."

I hung up, set about packing my bag and half an hour

later I went down, settled my bill and made for Teterboro Airport in New Jersey.

———

MEANWHILE, in Mexico, Joaquin Sanchez Martin was wondering who he would have to kill. His face, flushed under his deep tan, was an ugly purple color, his neck was swollen and his tendons looked like they were about to snap.

He was in the living room of the villa where Ismael Mario Zamora Garcia had been barely twenty-four hours earlier, and he was screaming into his cell phone.

"*Dead!*" he was screaming, "*Dead, dead, dead, dead! Everybody is dead!*"

On the other end of the line, Bill was saying, "I know, Joaquin, I'm watching it on the news."

"Ismael, *dead!* Francisco, *dead!* Sancho, *dead!* El Sicario, *dead! Thirty goddamn men in a couple of days! And El Jefe!*"

"I know, Joaquin, we are as shocked as you are, believe me."

His screams became shrill. "*You fockin' patronizin' me, you son of a bitch?*"

"No—"

"*You playin' me along? Tell him what he wants to hear?*"

"No—"

"*You tryin' to destroy the cartel, hijo de puta?*"

"No, listen to—will you listen to me?"

"*This is your puto CIA protection?*"

"*Ismael dead? Torn in half, hijo de puta! He was torn in half! His body was in the puto livin' room and his legs were in the yucca plant! This is what you call protection? Thirty men* dead in a couple of days! This is protection? Pendejo hijo de puta?"

"Now take it easy, Joaquin..."

"*Take it easy? Take it easy? You know what is gonna happen now? Every pendejo hijo de mala madre in Mexico is gonna be trying to move in on our territory! There is gonna be war! And what are you gonna do? Help the Gulf? Is that the new plan? Man you are dead! Dead! Mason is dead! The director of the CIA—you think he is safe in Langley? You think he is safe in Virginia? He is dead! Dead, man! Dead! You made a big mistake, Gringo, now you got a big problem!*"

He hung up and turned to look at the six men who were sitting and standing around the room, watching him. Four of them were hard, cruel-looking men in jeans and casual shirts. Of them one was clearly Indian, with long hair hanging loose down his back. Joaquin pointed at him. "Itzamatul, go to Culiacán, get Pedro Hoffman, bring him here. No telephone, no calls. Go, get him, bring him. I have jobs for you both."

The man they all knew as Itza, for short, rose and left the room. Of the other two, one was heavyset, with greedy blue eyes. He wore a leather jacket and Hugo Boss pants. The other was in his forties, though he looked younger. He wore a pale gray suit and eyes that never stopped calibrating and analyzing.

He pointed to the guy in the leather jacket. "Hans, you go to Los Mochis and you talk to Ortega, you tell him the gringos have betrayed us. Make him understand that if we fight each other now the other cartels will eat us for breakfast. Tell him we are meeting tomorrow night at the Manjar in Altata, to discuss how we respond to these attacks, and who takes over from Ismael."

He turned to the guy in the gray suit. "Diego, you take the helicopter and you go to Durango and you give the same message to Elisondo. Tomorrow night, I want everyone at the Manjar in Altata. You tell everyone, make sure they are there!"

Hans was pulling a pack of Marlboros from his leather jacket. He poked a cigarette in his mouth and fished a green disposable lighter from his pocket.

"What are you going to do?"

Joaquin's face flushed. "First, I'm gonna make sure every son of a bitch in Sinaloa is with us. Anyone who says no, dies tonight. If El Golfo, or any other son of a bitch tries to move in, we gonna massacre them. And then, I am gonna kill every *pendejo* gringo who has betrayed us. We gonna bomb the goddamn embassy and we are gonna go to Washington and kill the *hijo puta* director of the CIA!" His voice had been rising and now it became shrill again. *"They think they can do this to us? To us?"* He stabbed at his chest with his finger. *"To Sinaloa? They think they can kill Ismael Mario Zamora Garcia, and just walk away? They gonna die! All of them!"*

―――――

THE WOMAN DROVE ALL NIGHT. The colonel, in the passenger seat beside her, had his ankles manacled and his hands cuffed to the door. Cramps and shooting pains had kept him from sleep, but eventually sheer exhaustion had claimed him and drawn him into restless dreams.

It was a seventeen or eighteen-hour drive, but she had

taken it easy, not wanting to draw attention. Explaining to a Mexican cop why she had an American colonel manacled to the door of her car might have been challenging.

Just outside Hermosillo, before the railway bridge, she had pulled off the road and rolled down a shallow bank onto a dirt track. There was a guy waiting for her there in a dark blue Audi SR 5 Sportback with American plates. He jerked his chin at her and she said, "You know what Desmond said to Molly? He said, 'God, I like your face.'"

"And what did she do, take him by the hand?"

"Life goes on."

He had tossed her the fob and she had given him the keys to the truck. He had climbed in, killed the lights and disappeared among the trees and the undergrowth, and she had pulled back up the bank and continued on her way toward Tijuana and San Diego.

They crossed the border unimpeded in the small hours before dawn. She picked up the I-5 and headed for San Diego, and, as the horizon started to turn gray in the east, she took exit 17 and came off for San Diego International Airport. A complicated maze of roads took her finally to Grape Street, across the railway lines and onto the Pacific Highway, where she turned right and, after three blocks, pulled into the Motel 6 parking lot.

She killed the engine and pulled the cuff keys from her pocket. The colonel, who had been dozing fitfully, opened bleary eyes and looked at her.

"I really want you in one piece, Colonel, literally as well as figuratively. I am going to take your cuffs off. If you run, I will blow you in half, and there will be no way of tracing it to me. Understood?"

He grunted and stretched awkwardly. "Yeah, yadda yadda. Just take me somewhere I can lie down for a couple of hours."

She undid his cuffs and led him across the lot and up the steps to a room on the second floor. She knocked and a male voice said, "Yah?"

She said, "*Ewige Blumenkraft!*"

The door opened and a man in his fifties, with dark hair and dark eyes, let them in. The colonel pushed past them both, made for the bed and fell on it. Within seconds he was snoring softly. The man eyed him a moment and pointed to a chair by a table at the window. "Sit." She sat. He said, "You must be exhausted. You want a drink?"

"Yeah, later. Let's get the details sorted."

He went to the kitchenette and pulled a bottle of vodka and two shot glasses from a cupboard. He spoke as he went. His delivery was slow and precise.

"You are booked on the one thirty PM, Westjet to Calgary. The flight lands at five fifty. You are Mr. and Mrs. Henderson. You have a car waiting for you at the other end. It's not rented. It's yours. It's in the Indigo Parking Lot, third row, fifteenth car along, a silver Mercedes, the model and registration are in the envelope with your passports and all the rest of it."

He picked up a large, white envelope from beside the stove and dropped it on the table, before bringing over the glasses and the bottle. The woman ignored the drink and examined the contents of the envelope slowly and methodically.

"Passports, credit card for me," she glanced at the man, "not for him."

He smiled. "No, not for him. He might use it."

The corner of her mouth twitched. She went back to the contents of the envelope. "Driver's license for me, none for him, same reasoning..."

"Your address and telephone number are on your passports and on your driving license. Don't draw the cops' attention, don't get into any problems. Your fake IDs are paper thin and the minute they start poking around you'll be blown. This is enough to get you in and out of Canada, nothing more. When the job is done, you call me and we'll arrange your extraction. Any questions?"

She shook her head and drained her glass. She replaced it on the table and pushed it toward him for a refill. As he poured he said, "You have hand baggage in the wardrobe. Remember you fly at one thirty. You are already checked in, so you need to be going through security at twelve thirty the latest. Set your alarm for eleven thirty and get some sleep now. You have four hours. I'll watch the colonel."

She nodded. "OK, thanks."

She made her way to the bed and collapsed beside the colonel. Within thirty seconds she was snoring.

————

AND ONE THOUSAND three hundred miles north of where the woman lay snoring beside the snoring colonel, one thousand nine hundred miles north of where the two parts of Ismael Mario Zamora Garcia lay locked and frozen in a mortuary drawer, two thousand miles north of where Joaquin sat staring blindly at the wall with wild rage in his motionless eyes, and a good two thousand five hundred miles north of where Alex Mason sat hurtling at several hundred miles per hour along the runway at Mexico City's International Airport, Retired General Mike Ustinov sat watching CNN news on his TV in Calgary.

He watched the smoke billowing across the valley and the flames engulfing the house and the terrace of Zamora's villa. He had heard about Francisco Gallardo the day before, and he knew that whoever it was, was going to be coming for him next.

He smiled. That was fine. He would meet them on his terms and he would kill them. It was what he did. It was what he had always done. And if this time they got him, it was a better way to go than growing old and decrepit in a wheelchair.

He climbed the stairs to his den upstairs, opened his gun cabinet and began to select his weapons. Vaguely in his mind he thought of the Iron Duke, who had never lost a battle in his entire career. Always choose your battle, he had said, always choose your ground. He would choose his ground. He would take his RAM and drive up to Lake Louise, to his cabin above the Bow River, on the slopes of the Waputik Peak. Let them come for him there. He would be ready for them.

Let them come.

TWELVE

At six thirty in Calgary it was growing dark, and an icy wind was blowing out of the west, bringing the cold air down from the mountains. The woman found the Mercedes without difficulty, slung their bags in the trunk and slammed it shut. Then she turned to the colonel and smiled at him.

"So far, we have been in a lawless country, and I have been able to keep you chained up and relatively harmless. Now we are in Canada, the Denmark of the Americas, full of Lawful Larrys and Have-a-Go Harrys. That means the risk to my life just increased by one hundred percent, and the same goes for you, Colonel."

She jabbed her index finger on his chest.

"I need to explain something to you. My job is to take you to face trial. When you face trial I want you to be free of injury, so no one can say that you were tortured into confession. And I see the logic in that—" She paused and a thin smile touched his lips. She echoed the smile and went on,

"But that goes so far and no farther. If you try to run, I will shoot you, if you attack me, I will injure you, and if I see I can't stop you, I will blow you in half."

He stepped in close and his voice was somewhere between a purr and a growl. "Not if I have your arms pinned and you can't get at your phone."

Her eyes flicked over his face and she leaned into his ear and whispered, "It's as easy as, Siri, call Ian, and wherever you are in the world..."

He swallowed. She placed her finger on his chest and pushed. "Back up, Colonel, and thanks for the heads up. Get in the car."

He climbed in the passenger seat and she got behind the wheel.

They moved through the dense darkness. The snow had not started yet, but you could feel it in the air and in the low cloud cover. The streetlamps cast small pools of amber light that somehow made the darkness beyond them still deeper.

She avoided the highways and instead took 96th Avenue into town and threaded her way among suburban streets, occasionally making use of the Country Hills Boulevard when she had no other choice, until she came finally to Nose Hill Drive, which she followed south as far as the park office and then crossed over the freeway into the outer suburb of Tuscany. Here the lighting was still more sparse, and the darkness still deeper.

She turned right past the Home Depot and drove slowly north, following Tuscany Way for a little over a mile, then turned left onto the 12 Mile Coulee Road and out of the suburbs and into the darkness. Another turn and she was passing the golf links onto Bearspaw Village Road.

At a bend in the road the sweep of her headlamps picked out a large house on her right, perched at the top of a low hill, surrounded by tall pine trees. She said, "This is it," killed the lights and crawled in through the gate and up the drive to the house. The windows of the house were dark. She muttered to herself, "There's no car in the drive."

"Maybe in the garage."

She glanced at him. "Shut up." She opened the door. "Stay here."

She climbed out and walked over to the house. She peered through the windows and saw only dark, empty rooms. The drapes were open, so he had left during the day and had not returned.

She got back in the car, switched on the headlamps and rolled back onto Bearspaw Village Road. The nearest neighbor's drive was sixty feet away, and the house was a hundred yards down the drive. There she could see lights in the windows. She turned in and pulled up outside the house.

The door was opened by a big man in a cardigan with receding hair and reading glasses hung around his neck. In his hand he was holding a newspaper. On seeing strangers he raised his chin and contracted his brows.

"Do for ya?"

The woman smiled. "I am so sorry to disturb you. We are friends of Mike's," she turned and gestured toward the house, "we've come all the way from Washington—DC—not the state!" She laughed and got a smile. "We thought we'd surprise him for my birthday, but he's not in! Stupid of us, but we just assumed..."

"Young lady, I just know that when I tell him you came to see him and he wasn't here, he is going to kick himself.

But I am afraid he has gone up to his cabin, up at Lake Louise. He likes to go up there, commune with nature and do a little hunting." He smiled. "He's not too particular whether it's in season or not."

"Shoot, I should have thought of that. Stick that man between four walls for more than twenty-four hours and he starts growling."

"That's Mike. Look at me, keeping you on the doorstep in this cold. Won't you come in and have a drink?"

"Oh, that is so kind, but I am pooped from the journey. We'd better be getting back to the hotel, dinner bath and bed."

He smiled. "Well, don't you worry. I'll tell him you were here. He'll be mad as hell."

She returned to the car. Looking through the windscreen she could see the illuminated image of the man under the porch light, watching them. She fired up the engine, waved and smiled, and pulled out of the drive.

The colonel didn't even try to hide the smile in his voice. "He's up in his cabin, right? I could have told you that."

"You knew?" She glanced at him.

"Yeah, I guessed. But I was struggling to find one good reason why I should help you."

She didn't reply. She made her way down the 1A, looking for the McDonalds on 16th Avenue. There she bought four Big Macs and a gallon of coffee, before pulling out onto the Trans Canadian Highway 1, and heading west, toward the mountains.

At first they were silent as they moved through the city, watching the suburbs drift by in their chill, limpid light, but when they had crossed under the railway bridge, the colonel spoke. His voice was quiet, oddly cocooned in the cab.

"I am not stupid. I know what's happening."

He looked at her but she didn't answer. So he sighed and went on.

"You're a hit woman. Somebody panicked, probably in the Pentagon or in Langley." He eyed her and smiled. "You've got that Agency look about you." He looked away, at the sporadic cars passing on the far side. "My gamble was that any attempt made on my life would only serve to corroborate and confirm what was in the book. It made sense, but I see what you are trying to do."

She gave a small frown. "You do?"

"Sure, it's brutal, but if it were not too late, it might have worked. Kill enough people in a bloody enough way, and hold me hostage, you might just get the publisher to stop publication, and force me to recant and say the book is full of lies. That's the postscript you talked about." She didn't say anything. He smiled. "I'm not wrong, then. But I think you left it too late. You have, what, a month? There is no way they're going to stop the presses now."

After Calaway Park things started to get remote and the temperature started to drop. They passed the intersection at Exit 161, and she pulled into the Petro-Canada gas station to fill the tank. After that it became wilderness. They were a small, luminous bubble hurtling through a vast darkness. Pretty soon they began to climb. It was gradual at first, but by the time they had reached Cheneka, the gradients were steeper and the forests were denser. Another fifteen minutes and they had arrived at the exit for Seebe, and past that they started to climb into the wilds of the Rockies and a light snow began to fall. The colonel smiled.

"This is where it starts to get dangerous—"

"You keep telling yourself that, Colonel. You think it hasn't been dangerous till now, you are living in a fantasy."

"I meant the road." His tone was bland. "The snow is late. At this time of year these roads can become treacherous." She didn't answer. He went on, "What's your name?"

"Peggy Sue. I'm the girl next door every nice boy wants to marry. Daddy worked in the accounts department of a major American firm and Mom stayed at home and made apple pie."

"You're cute, funny."

"But then one day this big, bull of a guy—I don't know if he was Scottish or Irish or Welsh—one of those big Celtic types, with a neck like an ox, legs like tree trunks, pale blue eyes, real short hair, he decided he wanted to make out with me in the kitchen, while my dad was doing sums and my mom was hanging out the washing." She paused, watching the long black road snaking through the pool of light cast by her moving car, with the white dusting of flakes. She gave a small sigh. "He was much bigger and much stronger than me. He quickly overpowered me and threw me on the kitchen table. He climbed on top of me. He was so heavy I couldn't move. He kept telling me, 'Just let it happen, go with it.' I tried, I really tried to get out from under him, but his strength and his weight were so overwhelming, and he kept telling me to give in, to surrender..."

She looked at him. He was grinning. She smiled back, intimate and close in the confined space in the dark.

"So I took the vegetable knife my mom had been using

to cut the apples, and I rammed it three inches into the bastard's ass. You ever heard a pig scream when it's going to be killed? This was much worse. He tried to get off me but he couldn't stand with that big old knife in his ass. So he fell on the floor, and I went to work with my size eights. By the time I'd finished with his face, I don't think even his mother would have recognized him."

She turned to the colonel. He had stopped smiling. He'd turned away and was looking at his unhappy reflection in the window, against the blackness outside.

"I didn't kill that boy because my mom had heard the scream and come running in. But he had stopped even trying to protect himself. It's a miracle he didn't get brain damage."

There was a minute of silence, broken only by the hum of the engine. Then she glanced at him again and said, "You keep talking, Colonel, you keep trying like you think there's going to be some kind of reverse Stockholm Syndrome shit between us. But you need to understand something about me. I am not a nice person. I don't stop. I get the job done. What is the job? Kill Zamora. So I don't stop until Zamora is dead. Do twenty other collateral assholes get killed in the process? Read my lips—I don't care. What is the job? Bring Colonel Ian Cameron in dead or alive. So I don't stop until I bring you in, dead or alive. Are you suffering? Are you basically a nice guy? Read my lips, I-don't-care. And you can add to that the fact that I really don't like you. You remind me of the asshole on my mom's kitchen table. So if there comes a point where I have to shoot you, or blow you in half—"

"Yeah, I know, read your lips. You don't care."

"Got it."

"Sweet kid."

By the time they pulled into Lake Louise it was closing on ten o'clock. The snow had stopped and the sky was clear, but there were deep drifts and it was icy cold. The town was small and quiet. The Mountain Restaurant located beside the gas station was closed, but they rolled on down the Main Street and soon came to the Explorers Lounge. It was open and warm light from the doors and windows lay on the snow in the driveway and the parking lot. The woman pulled in and killed the engine.

"You know where his cabin is?"

"No, I was never invited. I did his dirty work, but we never socialized."

"That's heartbreaking. Now you listen to me. We go in, we have a burger, some pie and coffee, and I find out where the cabin is. Then we move on. One false move and I will cause you a lot of pain before I kill you."

"Yeah, I know. You're a real badass. Don't worry. I'm in no hurry to have my spine blown in half. I'll be good."

They stepped into the stone-clad porch and pushed through the glass doors into the warmth and light of the restaurant. Everything was wood and there was a soft murmur of polite, Canadian conversation. The woman walked up to the bar. The guy standing behind it smiled at her, but before she could speak the colonel said, "Say, pal, can you help us. We're going to eat, we're going to have a couple of wild boar burgers and a couple of beers, right honey?"

The woman grinned at him. "You betcha!"

"But help me out here. It's my wife's birthday—"

"Oh, well a happy birthday to you, and many happy returns."

She giggled and thanked him. The colonel pressed on. "But as a special birthday treat we decided to come up and surprise an old army buddy of mine—actually my commanding officer, but we became pals, and he also happens to be my wife's godfather—long story!"

While he'd been talking, the bartender had been pouring two beers and set them on the counter. The colonel continued.

"So he lives in Calgary?" He gave it the intonation of a question. "But when we showed up, he wasn't there. All the way from DC, can you beat that?"

"That's too bad. So is he up here?"

"That's what his neighbor says. He has a cabin up here. They said it was in the foothills of Waputik Peak, above the Bow River."

The man made a big elaborate nod and said, "Oooh, I know who you mean. Oh, yes. We know him well around here. We call him the general. I don't know if he is one, but he has that military air."

"No kidding!" The colonel laughed. "Well he is in fact a general, General Mike Ustinov."

"Mike, that's the man. He was here having lunch just this afternoon. Very polite and agreeable. And you want to get to his cabin tonight?"

The woman clenched her hands like she was praying. "We do! Before midnight, while it's still my birthday!"

"Are you accustomed to mountain roads?"

"Hey, I grew up in the Midwest, we both did, and I have

hunted Taliban in the mountains of Afghanistan. We'll be fine."

They all laughed, he gave them the burgers to go and gave them detailed directions on how to find the general's cabin in the dark. They thanked him and carried their food out to the car. When they had climbed in she narrowed her eyes at him.

"What the hell was that?"

He regarded her a moment and blinked once. "Do I look like a military man to you?"

"Does sh—"

"Yeah, OK, skip it. The point is it's going to look a lot more convincing, a guy like me looking for his army pal, than a beautiful woman like you looking for," he shook his head and shrugged, "Who? What? This is Neighborhood Watch country. These people look out for each other. I come in asking for him, that's normal. You come in asking for him, that's weird."

She nodded. "Don't every call me honey again."

"You're welcome."

"OK, let's go and kill this son of a bitch."

THIRTEEN

It was dark. There was no moon. But the narrow strip of sky between the black hulks of the mountains was translucent and peppered with icy stars. The forest was so dense and shrouded in snow to right and left I almost missed the turn. The gap in the woodland appeared as I was passing. I slammed on the brakes, reversed and saw a broad track that wound in among the trees. I spun the wheel of my rental Jeep and moved into the deep shadows.

I killed the lights and crawled along at fifteen miles per hour. The snow on the track was an eerie luminous blue. Under the snow the track was rutted and pitted from rain, snow and use, and the truck lurched and bumped as I moved along. Pretty soon it turned to the right and started to climb steeply. The big engine whined and ground on the increasingly steep gradient and I worried for a moment it might be heard, but I was pretty sure the giant, densely packed pines would absorb the sound.

And then, after ten or fifteen minutes, leaning out of the window I saw ahead that the track opened out into a snow-covered clearing. I dropped to little more than a couple of miles an hour and eased my way to the edge of the esplanade. I killed the engine and climbed out.

I was looking at a two-story cabin made of huge logs. The windows were dark and the silence was absolute. I stayed in the shelter of the trees and made my way around the house. There was no sign of life anywhere. That didn't mean he wasn't there. It just meant he wasn't showing signs of life. He might be in bed snoring, or he might be watching me through a telescopic sight. I was pretty sure he had seen the news, and he'd figured he might be next on the list, and that was why he'd come up to the cabin. If that was the case, a man like Ustinov would not be likely to allow himself to be caught with his pants down.

I approached the back door, which I assumed would open onto the kitchen. The lock was an old-fashioned Chubb, but two got you twenty there was at least one dead-bolt at the bottom of the door, and probably another at the top. I walked around to the front of the house and had a look at the door there. It was a Yale lock, and whether it had deadbolts or not was a moot point. I looked for signs of an alarm, but I was pretty sure there wouldn't be one. Out here, in such a remote place, it would be an unnecessary expense. And the general, like most people who lived on the fringes of the law, would probably prefer not to have the restraining influence of the cops present while he dealt with an intruder.

I pulled the Maxim 9 from under my arm and blew out the lock. In spite of the internal suppressor and the subsonic rounds, in that extreme silence the report, and the impact of the slug on the lock, were loud.

I waited, counting steadily to sixty. Nothing happened, and I heard nothing inside the house. I hunkered down beside the door and pushed it gently open with my outstretched arm. Still nothing happened. So I slipped inside and flattened myself against the wall. Then I hunkered down, closed my eyes and counted to one hundred and twenty, allowing my senses to creep through the house like mist, trying to capture the slightest movement or sound.

When I opened them again they had adjusted to the darkness and I could make out a large room with a huge fireplace, a big staircase made of hewn logs and a galleried landing on the second floor. Then I became aware of the subtle scent of wood ash.

I stood and moved into the room. The voice came calm and steady, not shouting or screaming, simply making a calm statement.

"Put your weapon on the floor, Mr. Mason, then place your hands in the air. I don't especially want to kill you, though I have a perfect right to do so, and I shall, without hesitation, if you give me cause."

I cursed myself silently, and had to admit to a certain admiration for a man who was capable of remaining perfectly still and silent in those conditions. I scanned the shadows, but couldn't find him. I raised my hands, bent forward and placed the Maxim 9 on the floor.

"It may not look like it," I said, "but I am actually here to help you."

"You're quite right. It doesn't look like it. If a man enters my house at night, secretly and carrying a gun, I am not inclined to believe he's there to help me."

"Have you seen the news recently?"

"Mm-hmm—"

"So you've seen that Zamora and Gallardo were murdered."

"I saw that, yes."

"I figured they would come for you next, seeing as you were Cameron's handler."

"I figured that too, which is why I am holding a gun on you right now."

"I work for the government, General. I am not a professional assassin. If you'd care to think about it for a moment, I didn't know what I was going to find when I got here. We have a file on you and we knew about this cabin, so we figured this was where you were most likely to be. But if we knew that, your prospective assassin probably knew it too. When I got here everything was closed and dark..." I shrugged and trailed off.

There was a silence that was uncomfortably long. Then there was a sigh. "Close the door, will you? Put a chair up against it or something."

I pushed the door closed, found a straight-backed chair behind it and wedged it closed. Then a lamp snapped on behind me. He was sitting in a big, leather armchair beside the fireplace. The chair was big enough to obscure his silhouette in the dark. He had a Desert Eagle in his hand, resting in his lap. He used it to point to a chair opposite his on the other side of the fireplace. I went to it and sat.

"So you're not the undertaker."

"No, I work for the Office of the Director of Intelligence. We don't carry out assassinations. The CIA Special Activities department takes care of that."

"ODIN. I've heard about you. You didn't exist in my day. So what do you take care of?"

"As the name suggests, we gather and collate intelligence, and if we identify a threat to national security, we address it."

He chuckled. "Speaking of intelligence, do I look stupid to you?" He didn't and I shook my head. "I'm not. I have a very big ego, and I like to win, so I decided to join MENSA. You know what MENSA is, right? It's a club for geniuses. A genius is anyone with an IQ of more than one hundred and forty-five."

"So you're a genius..." It wasn't a question, more of a statement of skepticism.

"I have an IQ of one hundred and sixty. Of course, your IQ fluctuates. You have a lower IQ when you have the flu, or a hangover. You have a higher IQ after a cold shower while listening to Mozart."

"Congratulations. Is this relevant to anything?"

"Yeah, I'm letting you know I'm not stupid."

"Good, that will help. I left Mexico immediately after Zamora was killed. It's a fair guess Zamora's assassin did too. So if I am here now, your exceptional intellect should be telling you there is somebody close behind me who intends to kill you."

He smiled. "I'm about as worried as I am stupid. You know something that pisses me off?"

"Men who wear their trousers below their ass? Women who wear their hair in front of their face? General, there is somebody on their way up to Lake Louise who aims to kill you. And if the last couple of days are anything to go by, that person is extremely good at what they do."

It was like he hadn't heard me. "It's the misuse of the word, *dimension*. Everybody does it, even people who should know better. Thy talk about dimensions like a dimension was a parallel reality or universe. Have you noticed that? They talk about how there may be lots of dimensions all over the place, so small we can't see them, or circular, wrapped in on themselves. But they never stop to think, however much you twist 'em, however small they are, they are still within the three dimensions of space. That's what happens when you over-sophisticate things."

I sighed. He plowed on. "Do you know, Mason, what a dimension is?"

"A parallel universe or reality?"

"A dimension is simply something you can measure. Space has three of them—up-down, across and depth. Those are the three measurable dimensions of space. Time is another way of measuring space. Time measure change and movement in space. So Einstein said time was the fourth dimension of space. But he was wrong."

"Einstein was wrong."

He sat forward with his elbows on his knees and the Eagle held loosely in both hands. His eyes were watching my face carefully.

"Weight—"

"Wait?"

"Gravity. Gravity, like time, is a product of space. Three-dimensional space is a cube, right? And anything contained in that tube is going to tend to press in on itself. We can measure that pressure, so gravity, not time, is the fourth dimension of space."

"What the hell are you talking about, General? There is somebody—"

"You'll notice that the dimensions of space become progressively more subjective. Time is the fifth dimension and, as relativity shows, has a strong subjective element. Pain, which is a product of tension, which is another consequence of three-dimensional space, is another way of measuring space, but it is much more subjective than time. Contract, suffer, relax, enjoy."

"General..."

"I am trying to tell you something here, Mason. But all you can think about is this asshole who wants to kill me. That is his problem, not mine."

"You're trying to tell me you discovered the fourth or fifth or sixth dimension of space. Congratulations. You're a genius. Now I need to take you back to DC, and we need to get moving."

His smile said he was both incredulous and disappointed.

"You think I am going to go back to DC with you?" He shook his head. "You haven't been listening. This..." He waved his hand around the huge room. "All of this, from objective reality to subjective experience, is all governed by immutable laws that are woven into the very fabric of three-dimensional space."

"You're out of your mind, General. What the hell are you talking about?"

"Things are what they are. I can no more walk away from this fight, than you could float off the surface of the planet. All I can do is choose my battleground, and meet them when they come."

"That's bullshit. You can come with me, get in my Jeep and come back to DC with me."

He shook his head again. "It's like the dimensions. However much you shrink or twist them, they are still up-down, across and deep. Gravity must press into the center of mass, time must flow when things move in space. Everything is what it is. I could come with you to DC, assuming you're not here to kill me. But then I wouldn't be me." He shrugged. "And what would you gain, anyhow? Postpone my death by a few years, so that I can live out my last decade in prison? Swap one kind of death for another? Nah. Besides, aren't you curious to find out who is doing this? I am. It's sure as hell not the Company." He pointed at me. "And a more pertinent question: *why?* What are they doing it for? These are grudge killings, but on a grand scale. I am curious."

I leaned forward, staring hard into his eyes. "You're a military man, for Christ's sake. These people took out Zamora's villa, in the heart of Sinaloa, protected by a small army—and they took it out with what seems to have been a thermobaric missile. Think like a soldier, for crying out loud! You think you can take them on sitting here with a Desert Eagle and a broken door? They'll kill us both before we even know they're here."

"I'm not a soldier. I'm a CIA officer, and like most CIA officers, I am out of my mind. You are welcome to leave any time you like."

I stood and went and picked up my Maxim 9 and tucked

it under my arm. I looked at him a moment and sighed. "I'm not leaving."

He shrugged. "Don't expect me to be grateful."

"No, I won't expect that. Do you know who this is? Do you know who's doing it?"

"No."

"Do you suspect, have a hunch, speculate?"

He seemed to think about it. "No. I know what you know, Mason. The logical thing is that we should all be whistling at the sky and making like we know nothing, and hope Ian will just go away. Executing him is in nobody's interest. So the answer is no, I have no idea. But I'd sure love to find out."

There was a noise. It was indistinct and its location was hard to pinpoint. But it was a noise. I looked toward the back of the house and he smiled.

"A bad tactician would now withdraw either to the upper floor or the basement. That would buy us time, but cost us our freedom of movement. What we want to do, when they arrive, is bring them into the cabin while we exit to the exterior."

The noise came again, like a distant, high-pitched whine. I frowned and he said, "They are boarding up the back door, so we can escape. Maybe they plan to burn the house and shoot us as we attempt to escape."

I felt a sudden surge of anger at the thought that I was going to die in this place for no good reason, simply because of this man's stupid obstinacy. Before I could say anything there was a hammering on the front door. I frowned at the general, but he remained impassive. Then a man's voice bellowed:

"General Mike Ustinov, do you recognize my voice? Do you know who I am?"

The general didn't answer. The voice bellowed again.

"It's me, Ian. I have a gun stuck to my head, General. And I am instructed to give you this message. If you come out in the next fifteen minutes and allow yourself to be taken into custody, your life will be spared. If not, in fifteen minutes and one second all hell will break loose and you, and whoever was driving the Jeep, will die a horrific, violent death. Make your choice."

General Mike Ustinov stood and took a few paces toward the door. Then he hunkered down and shouted, "Ian! It's been a long time. I thought you had more guts than this. I thought you'd choose to die on your feet, kicking ass. Who's got you? Who took you?"

"I dunno, Mike. They won't tell me, but they are well equipped and well trained. My money is on the Agency. But if you ask me why the Agency is killing off cartel members, I gotta tell you, I have no idea."

The general remained hunkered down a moment, then called out, "How many of them are there?"

He was answered by a stifled cry of pain, and a moment later, slightly breathless, "All I can tell you, Mike, is the clock is ticking. You'd better come out, these people mean business. Who's in there with you?"

He looked at me along his eyes, the shook his head and said, "Nobody. It's just me in here."

"You've got seven minutes, Mike, then they're going to take you out with RPGs. If you have someone in there with you, you should let them leave now, Mike."

Then there was silence, and I noticed for the first time

the ticking of a grandfather clock up against the wall, beside the fire.

They didn't wait till the fifteen minutes were up. Something, call it intuition or a hunch, or just plain experience, made me shift suddenly. I took a big stride, grabbed the general by the scruff of his neck and dragged him staggering back toward the kitchen. It was just a second later that the windows shattered and two grenades tumbled in.

Explosions, unless there is a lot of liquid fuel involved, are not like they are in the movies. There is no thundering roar, and no billowing fireball. Most explosions are nasty, flat smacks. They last a fraction of a second, jar your bones and your ears and make you feel sick, if they don't tear you to pieces. I hurled the general into the kitchen, slammed the door and threw myself on the ground, covering my ears with my hands. A moment later that horrible clap shook the house and the door was ripped off its hinges and hurled across the room, taking the breakfast table and four chairs with it.

I stood. The room spun and I searched through the dust and smoke for the general. He was on his knees, struggling to get to his feet.

Staggering, trying to keep the floor from rising up to smack me in the head, I grabbed one of the shattered chairs and hurled it through the window, tearing the red and white gingham curtains in the process and shattering the glass. A blast of cold air hit me in the face and I dropped, expecting a hail of hot lead from whoever was outside, watching the back.

Instead I heard the front door being kicked in. I pulled

the Maxim from under my arm and snarled at the general. "Out! The window! Now!"

He staggered a couple of steps and fell on his hands and knees. I pressed up against the doorjamb, dropped to my haunches, spun and let off four rounds at the front door. As I ducked back four shots ripped into the doorframe. I looked at the general. He was still on all fours, reaching up for the window frame, but he was faltering. I ran to him, grabbed him by his belt and his collar and heaved. He didn't help much, but I managed to get him half out the window, then grabbed his ankles and heaved him out. I turned, fired five shots at the door and clambered out the window and landed in a small snowdrift beside the general. He was groaning and I saw for the first time he had a trickle of blood oozing out of his ear. I swore violently, hooked my arm under his armpit and rasped, "*Run, you son of a bitch! Run!*"

We half ran, half staggered to the corner of the cabin, with the general stumbling and falling every two or three steps. I peered round the corner and saw faint starlight reflecting off the hood of my Jeep behind the trees. Out in the open, making no attempt to remain hidden, was a silver Mercedes. I was taking aim at the front tire when a thud behind me made me turn.

There was a woman standing holding a gun in both hands, aiming at the general. He was on his hands and knees and let out a weird mix of a snarl and a shout, "*No!*" He grabbed my arm and planted his right foot on the ground. "I will not die on my knees."

He struggled, groaning, and got to his feet. His cheek was smeared with blood from his ear. I said, "For God's sake, this man needs a doctor."

The woman kept her eyes fixed on the general, her feet apart and her arms stretched out in front of her. She said, "This is not your fight, Mason. Walk away. Get in your Jeep and leave."

I narrowed my eyes, screwed up my brow. "What?"

"This has nothing to do with you. Get the hell out of here!"

"*Gallin...?*"

FOURTEEN

I DIDN'T HAVE TIME TO PROCESS WHAT I WAS seeing and hearing. Suddenly the general was bellowing like a wounded bull, "*Come on! Do it! Finish it! Shoot me dead!*" He pounded his chest with his fists. "*Who the hell wants to grow old anyway. Shoot for Chrissakes! Pull the goddamn trigger!*"

As he was bellowing I was watching Colonel Ian Cameron climbing laboriously out of the kitchen window. Gallin was shouting at me, "I'm serious, Mason. Get the hell out of here!"

The colonel came up behind Gallin and I realized too late what he was going to do. I stepped forward, shouting, "*No! Gallin!*" The colonel swung his fist. Gallin squeezed the trigger. Her gun exploded and spat fire. The colonel's fist smashed into the back of her head. The general's head whiplashed and blood and gore erupted from the back and sprayed over the luminous white snow.

I swore, "*Jesus!*" and next thing I was running and the

colonel was on his knees, grabbing the weapon from Gallin's fingers. I was six feet away and the cannon was pointing at me. I stopped. He snarled, "Keep back. I am not going to hurt anyone, but take one step closer and you both die."

"Take it easy, Colonel. We don't want anybody else to die."

He grinned without humor and got down on one knee beside Gallin. "Yeah, we can agree on that much. Just back up a bit while I get her cell."

I backed up half a step with one foot while he reached in her pocket. "You want to tell me what the hell is going on? I've been searching for you all over the damned continent."

He stood and slipped her phone in his pocket.

"Maybe when you find out you can explain it to me. You a cop?"

I shook my head. "I'm with a special department of the Pentagon."

"Yeah, well..." He pointed down at Gallin, who was starting to groan. "I don't know who the hell this bitch is, who her damned friends are or who she works for. But whatever she tells you, I have not killed anybody. I could have taken her out right now, I could take you both out, but I didn't. You see that, right? And she has given me reason. Last couple of days she has killed my closest friends, guys who were like brothers to me. But I am letting it go."

I nodded. "OK, that's good."

"Don't fuckin' patronize me. When this is over, I want to enjoy the proceeds of my damn book. Now I am gonna tell you what we are going to do. You're going to give me the keys to the Jeep. I am going to take the Mercedes, and at the end of the track I am going to drop the keys out the window.

By the time you get there and find them, I'll be on my way back home. And you, if you work for the Pentagon, get this homicidal bitch locked up! She's out of her mind."

Gallin was pushing herself up, getting to her knees. The colonel strode a few steps, then stopped and turned. He pointed at her again. "Don't let her anywhere near a phone. You know what she did?" He took a step closer. "You know what she did? She injected C4 into my back, with a nano-chip detonator. She makes a phone call and I explode. She says to me, if she doesn't make the call, her office can call me anywhere in the world. I'm tellin' you. She's out of her mind. Don't let her anywhere near a phone till I've got this damned thing out of me. Promise me that!"

I nodded. "Yeah."

He nodded back and walked away. I turned to Gallin. She was scowling at his retreating form from under her brows. As he disappeared around the corner I said, "What the hell are you doing, Aila?"

Then there was a blur and she was sprinting after him. He was armed, she wasn't. I couldn't shout. All I could do was go after her. I scrambled to my feet and reached the corner of the building as she rugby tackled him to the snow. He went down with a big *whoof!* And she was climbing on his back, pounding his head and trying to wrestle the Sig Sauer from his hands. I bellowed at her, "*Gallin! For Christ's sake!*"

I wrapped my arms around her and dragged her off. She was kicking her legs and screaming at me to let her go. I bellowed at her to keep still but she ignored me. The colonel was groaning and I saw the Sig in the snow a few inches from his fingers. I kicked Gallin's feet from under her, threw her in the snow, stepped over and grabbed the Sig.

When I turned back Gallin was on her feet again, glaring at me.

"Mason, this is not—"

"Shut up!"

I turned back to the colonel and snapped, "Get up!"

He got painfully to his feet and gave Gallin a dangerous glare. I bellowed, "*Enough! Both of you!*"

I avoided the comical aspect of the situation by remembering how many people had died, and the general's body lying in the snow just around the corner. And though he was an unmitigated son of a bitch, in the short conversations we had had, I'd got the feeling there was a human being in there, somewhere. He had at the least deserved a trial.

"Now I am going to tell you what is going to happen next. This madness ends now. *Right now!* We are going to get in the Jeep." To Gallin I said, "You got cuffs?" She nodded. "So I am going to cuff you to the rear passenger door. You are done killing for this season. And you, Colonel, are going to drive us to the clinic in Lake Louise, where they are going to remove the explosive from your back. After that we are going to go to Calgary from where you are going to fly home, and I am going to take the colonel to DC with me. After that you can expect formal protests and representations at a diplomatic level. What the *hell* were you thinking?"

She didn't answer. She just stared at the colonel.

"Get me the cuffs, Gallin."

"Screw you." She said it without averting her eyes from

the colonel. I turned to him and said, "Get behind the wheel, Colonel, and close the door."

He climbed behind the wheel and slammed the door. I walked up to Gallin and she finally looked at me.

"I am not going to ask you for an explanation, not now. But even you must see that this has got out of control. I am not going to take you in. I'm not sure I'm even going to tell Nero what's happened here. Get on a plane, go to Israel or London, and I will make this go away. But stop, already." She nodded. I said, "Give me the cuffs, even if it's just for show."

She closed her eyes and sighed.

"OK."

I followed her across the snow to the Mercedes. She opened the driver's door, pulled a set of cuffs from the glove compartment and handed them to me.

"I should have cuffed him after I made him call the general." She shrugged. "But there was no time. I had to act fast and I thought the threat of the explosive in his back would keep him in line. Important lesson. Never underestimate your opponent."

We walked to the Jeep and I opened the rear door furthest from the driver. I said, "Get in. I'm going to cuff you to the door."

A long, thick, silver needle of pain pierced my head with violent suddenness. For a fraction of a second the universe was a black place with a gleaming, chrome shaft of agony running through it.

And then there was nothing.

I was freezing. I was in the North Pole, shivering, with icy water creeping over my skin, and the frozen air penetrating into my joints. I searched for the duvet to cover me and protect me from the snow, felt my face, numb and wet, and emerged into reality. Pain lanced through my brain and for a moment I thought I was going to vomit. I pushed myself to my knees, then did a balancing act till I was on my feet. The world tipped and I held on to the Jeep till it had stopped swinging and moving.

I felt my head. "What the hell did she hit me with?" I looked around, realized there was nobody there to answer me, and figured I was still mildly delirious.

I climbed behind the wheel, feeling weak and sleepy, and saw that my hands were trembling. "Hypothermia," I said aloud, and pressed the starter button. The engine rumbled reassuringly. I waited a couple of minutes for the cab to start warming up, and for my body to start settling down. "It's all ups and downs," I told myself, and wondered at Gallin beating me over the head. "Son of a gun," I muttered, and was surprised at how sad I felt.

I turned the Jeep around and started the steady roll down toward the main road. I felt for my cell and saw it had no signal. A twist of anxiety gripped my gut and I wondered if the colonel realized that as long as he was up here, he was safe. Then I felt my head and wondered if that was after all an accurate assessment of the situation.

I [passed through a silent, empty Lake Louise and continued descending out of the mountains toward Calgary. There was no sign of the silver Mercedes anywhere. Not only would the car be faster than the Jeep, but the driver would have a much clearer head.

By the time I'd passed the exit for Cheneka my signal came back. I hesitated a moment, then called Nero.

"Have you any idea what time it is, Alex?"

"No. I am driving down from the Rockies. I have a bad headache and I think I might be in the early stages of hypothermia."

He sighed and I heard him sit up. "What do you want me to do?"

I screwed up my face, and after a moment I said, "Think. I need you to think for me."

"Good grief."

"Shut up. Sir. Let me tell you. I found the general in his cabin. He refused to come with me and the hit man showed up while we were arguing. They lobbed grenades into the house."

"They?"

"See, that's what I mean. I need you to think for me. Sir, this has to stay strictly between you and me."

"What does?"

"The hit man, 'they,' was Aila Gallin."

"I feared as much."

"You *knew?* And you sent me...?"

"Calm down. I had no idea it was Aila Gallin, but I suspected it might be the Mossad."

"But..."

"I'll explain when you come in. What happened?"

"She killed the general. Then the colonel knocked her unconscious."

"So he was with her. He is still alive?"

"I think so. He knocked her unconscious and refused to kill her, or me. But as he was leaving she tackled him and brought him down. I managed to take control of the situation for a couple of minutes, but she knocked me cold from behind. I guess she suckered me. When I came round she was gone, with the colonel."

He sighed noisily. "When will men learn that you can't trust women. You know what Freud said about women?"

"Something about an undiscovered country. Tell me some other time, sir. What do I need to do?"

"I will have a word with Anthony and we will make representations to Gilad. Meanwhile I will talk to Gabriel, Aila's father, and see if we can iron this out. Meanwhile, find a good hotel, have a sleep and a meal and take the Gulfstream to Tel Aviv. I very much fear the colonel is to be tried and executed."

"Sweet Jesus—"

"I doubt he can help you. This is Elohim business, very much Old Testament."

"OK." I hung up. I drove on in silence, winding down the long, empty road. Eventually I snapped, "Siri! Call Gallin!"

I heard it ring and felt a hot twist in my gut. It rang five times and was cut short. She'd hung up.

The Doubletree Hilton was on 16th Avenue, which was what the Trans Canada Highway was called when it cut through the center of Calgary. I called, told them it was an emergency and asked if they had a room. They told me they had and, an hour later I collapsed onto the bed and was just sinking into a deep, restless sleep when my phone jangled me awake. I sat up and fumbled for the device and put it to my ear.

"Yeah, Mason."

There was a silence that went on a little too long, then Gallin's voice asked me, "Where are you?"

I made three false starts before I finally said, "I should tell you I am dying of hypothermia in the snow."

"I wouldn't believe you. I know how tough you are."

"That won't work."

"Where are you? The Doubletree?"

I frowned. "How...?"

"It's obvious. It's big enough to have rooms at this time of year, and it's right on the highway, for you to get going in the morning. I'm sorry I hit you."

"Yeah, me too. It hurts."

"You're tough. Eggs and bacon. The protein will do you good."

"Gallin, what the hell are you doing?"

"I'm calling to tell you to forget about this. You didn't see me. I was never there. We will never discuss this. It has nothing to do with you and me."

"You know that's impossible."

"No, Mason. You know that is exactly what is going to happen. Let it go, Mason. I'll call you soon. We'll go and have oysters and Guinness in Dublin. I'm sorry I hit you," she said again. "I'll make it up to you, I promise."

And with that she hung up.

I felt hollow and unhappy. I went to the bathroom and brushed my teeth. Then I had a shower. I still felt unhappy. So I went back to the bedroom, threw my clothes on a chair and fell into bed. I sank quickly into a deep, dark place. It wasn't freezing anymore, but there was somebody frowning at me. He had a bald head and very round blue eyes, and he was asking, "Who are you now?"

There was a beach over on the right, with luminous turquoise water and gleaming white sand. Gallin's voice called to me, "I can't really make it up to you in Dublin, can I?"

I shook my head slowly and her face was very close to mine. "I have to go to Tel Aviv. You know I have to go to Tel Aviv."

She said, "No," and I woke up. I lay looking at the pale gray window. It was morning. I sat up and swung my legs out of bed. I grabbed my cell and called Nero.

"Alex."

"Sir, I need to pull out. I am too personally connected with Gallin. There could be a conflict of loyalties. You should send somebody else."

"Very well, but before I do perhaps I should tell you that intelligence which reached me this morning indicates a Sinaloa team is on its way to Israel. Somehow they have acquired information which implicates Aila Gallin in Zamora's murder."

"Hell—"

"Shall I appoint another agent?"

"No, no I'll go. I'm on my way."

I got dressed, grabbed my bag and started to pack.

FIFTEEN

IT WAS A LONG, TIRING BUT UNEVENTFUL JOURNEY, and almost twenty-four hours later I handed the bellboy twenty bucks, closed the door and walked out onto the balcony of the Vista Hilton in Tel Aviv and looked out at the breakers in the late afternoon light, crashing onto the shores of the Hilton beach. No sooner had I leaned my forearms on the balustrade than my cell rang. The screen told me it was the office.

"Yeah, Mason."

Lovelock's dark chocolate voice with a hint of cinnamon answered.

"I'm not even going to flirt with you. The chief wants to talk to you ten minutes ago."

"OK, Lovelock. Put him through."

A second later Nero's peremptory voice snapped, "Mason."

"Sir—"

"I have spoken to Gabriel, and to just about everybody

at our end and theirs, including the president. What we discussed is confidential and I cannot share it with you, ever. But what emerged is this, that, given certain conditions, everybody wants this to go away."

He waited for my response. I gazed at the hazy, turquoise horizon, trying to visualize the southeastern shore of Crete. It was an act of faith, believing what I could not see or measure. I thought vaguely of the general and his dimensions. Nero's voice nagged at my ear.

"Alex?"

"Yes, sir, I was just wondering if that was a good thing."

"Unless..." He stopped himself. "Trust me, Alex, it is a good thing."

"I'll take your word for it. You are a genius, I am not. So what happens now?"

"Good of you to notice. What happens now? In the next hour your friend Aila Gallin will collect you from your hotel. She will take you to a meeting. They will hand over the colonel to you—I am told the C4 has been removed from his spine—and you will bring him back to the United States, to the Washington which is in the District of Columbia."

"That one, fine. Sir?"

"Yes—"

"What happened? What the hell was all this about."

"Nothing happened, Alex. I just told you that. It wasn't about anything, because nothing happened."

I sighed. "Fine, I'll keep you posted."

"Do."

He hung up.

Forty minutes later reception called to say that Captain

Gallin was waiting for me in the lobby. I pulled on my jacket, rode the elevator down and stepped out into the bright, crowded lobby. I didn't recognize her at first. She was standing by the door in jeans and a black leather jacket. Her hair was pulled back into a ponytail and she had no makeup on. The message was clear. She wasn't here to flirt or play games.

I walked over to her and she turned to look at me as I approached. I gave her an unhappy smile. "Of all the gin joints in all the towns in all the world..."

Her smile was as unhappy as mine. "How's your head?"

"I'll live. Fortunately you hit the hollow bit."

She turned away and looked at the bright sunshine outside, the taxicabs and the people climbing out of a small minibus. "You shouldn't be involved in this."

"Form what I am told there is no this to be involved in. It's like you said—or didn't say—it never happened."

She looked back and examined me with narrowed eyes. "If I ask you to, will you go away?"

I shook my head. "You know I can't. I have to take the colonel back with me." Something about her expression made me add, "That is the agreement."

"Yeah, that's the agreement. But not everybody agrees with the agreement."

"You?"

"I agree with the agreement, Mason. If it's honored on all sides."

She suddenly pushed off the wall and pushed her way through the revolving doors. I followed her. Outside, in the bright sunshine, she made her way to a dark blue Land Rover and climbed in, behind the wheel. I got in the passenger side. She fired up the engine and pulled away, toward Eliezer Peri Street.

"Are you telling me somebody might try to take me out?"

She glanced at me, held my eye for a moment and said nothing. We pulled onto the busy road and joined the flow of the traffic. I said:

"OK, so there is just one thing I need to know. If somebody, or a group of people, are going to try and take me out, are you with them?"

Her expression didn't change. "Don't be stupid. You're my friend. You're my family. Besides, I believe in the rule of law. I have my instructions and my mission, and I plan to seem them through."

"As long as I can count on you not to brain me again, that's what I plan to do."

She was quiet for a moment, then, "Brain you? I thought you said it never happened."

"That's what I've been told. I'm not sure General Mike Ustinov would agree."

"I can't comment on that."

"You can't comment?" I snorted. "You mean you're not allowed to comment. The general *can't* comment. You mayn't comment."

"Yeah, that's what I mean. I mayn't."

We seemed to be following a random pattern of twists and turns through the city. I asked her, "Are we actually going anywhere?"

"Yeah, eventually."

"So what are we doing right now?"

"Talking."

"About what never happened."

"Yeah." She glanced at me. "You almost killed me."

"*I* almost killed *you?*"

"You shot at me."

"Yes, but I didn't know it was you. You also shot at me."

"Right. I'm not blaming or recriminating. I'm just saying it was very intense." She glanced at me again, as though trying to read my face, see if I was understanding her. I frowned to show I wasn't. She sighed.

"I'm..." She stopped and started again. "I'm...*fond* of you. I, you know, you're like family. It's—" She looked at the traffic in all directions and turned onto Rabin Square. "It's not good that we should be shooting at each other."

"I'd have to agree. Gallin, what are you trying to say?"

"No." She shook her head. "No, not all. I am not trying to say anything. We are friends. Very good friends and we should not shoot at each other. That is all I am trying to say, Mason. Don't, don't, don't..."

"Don't what?"

"Anything." She looked at me and her eyes flitted over my face. "It's getting late. We'd better get to the meeting."

"Well, I'm glad we could have this little talk," I said, frowning.

"Me too. You OK?"

"Yeah."

"Good. We OK?"

"Yeah, Gallin, we're OK."

"Good."

Dusk was turning to evening and the streetlights and headlamps were coming on, washing the city with amber. We had been traveling down Frishman Street and now turned into Ben Yahuda. I said, "Tell me where we are going, Gallin."

"We are going to meet Lieutenant Colonel Ben Silverman. He will hand Colonel Ian Cameron over to you. I will escort you to the airport and you will leave Israel."

She took a right down toward the beach. It looked familiar. I said, "Yeah, but where?"

"Tayo Beach, it's pretty quiet this time of the year, this time of night."

"Tayo Beach?" The name rang a bell. I watched the four and five-story, dilapidated apartment blocks slip by. We took a couple of turns and emerged onto the seafront, with the beach on our right. We cruised past the tall palms, silhouetted against the deep blue of the sea and the evening sky.

"I've been here before," I said[1].

"Yeah? I didn't know that."

"I was looking for a friend."

Something in my tone of voice made her turn and look at me. For a moment she looked shockingly young, almost a child. Her eyes were pleading, frightened, vulnerable. It lasted a fraction of a second and she looked back at the road.

"Yeah? Who was that?"

"You. They kept telling me to accept you were dead. You weren't dead. You were in Iran. I knew you weren't dead."

"That was here?"

"Yeah, they took me to a stretch of wasteland near the beach and tried to kill me."

After a while she said, "I'm taking you to a plot of wasteland by the beach, but I don't plan to kill you, Mason."

We moved through light and shadow in a steady pulse. I looked at Gallin's face and thought for the millionth time that she was possessed of a special kind of beauty. We passed Banana Beach and then bore right toward Old Jaffa. We crossed Yossi Carmel Square and turned out along the Jaffa Port Road. We twisted and turned down narrow roads and a sense of misgiving began to grow inside me.

Then suddenly we were out of the old town on a brightly lit avenue and I knew exactly where we were.

"It's the same place," I said.

She frowned a moment, then shook her head. "Don't worry about it. It's just a convenient place to do business."

We eventually came to the beach. We were outside the city. I could see tower blocks on our left, beyond a broad stretch of wasteland. On the right there were palm trees and low sand dunes.

Gallin slowed and turned into a rough, improvised parking lot. We jerked and bounced over the rough ground. Ahead I could see another Land Rover that was parked in the shadow of a small beach bar which stood silent and dark. Here she killed the engine. I said, "It's exactly the same place. They brought me here to execute me."

"Relax. Nobody is going to execute you." Then she added, "Not so long as I'm here."

A couple of car doors slammed. I looked and saw two men had climbed out of the Land Rover. One of them stood holding an assault rifle. The other approached and opened my door. He said, "Mar Mason?"

"Yeah."

"I am Lieutenant Colonel Ben Silverman." He glanced past me. "Captain." To me he said, "You will please take the wheel and drive. Captain, you will take the passenger seat. Follow us, please."

I felt a stab of irritation. I said, "Yeah, sure. Where is Colonel Ian Cameron?"

He looked at me like he'd decided he didn't like me. "Just follow us, Mr. Mason, and Colonel Cameron will be handed over to you."

I got out, Gallin slipped over and I walked around and got behind the wheel. Colonel Silverman returned to his own vehicle, the armed guard got back in, his lights came on and I followed them out of the parking lot and onto the 431. The drove at speed as far as Modi'in Maccabim-Re'ut, some twenty miles inland from the beach. We drove through the town, then turned right onto Highway 443 and started heading east, climbing slowly into the hills.

Seven miles out of town we slowed and turned left onto a broad dirt track and we started to climb more steeply through the dark among sparse trees that might have been oaks or olives, it was hard to tell in the growing darkness. And after several hairpin bends we eventually came to a much smaller track on the left. The lead car turned onto it and I followed, and we moved slowly along the track in complete darkness. All I could see ahead were the red taillights of the truck ahead, and the circle of yellow light from his head-lamps. To left and right were the vague, stunted shapes of trees, and the jagged edges of sierra-like hills against the sky.

After five minutes the colonel's truck pulled up outside an old, ramshackle house and killed the lights. I pulled in behind him and saw an ancient, heavy wooden door open in the house. The dim, wavering light of candles or lamps spilled out and the silhouette of a man stood in the doorway, with his shadow stretching long and distorted across the yard.

Gallin said, "Don't get out."

I watched Silverman swing down from the cab and walk to the black silhouette in the doorway. He spoke to him for a moment and they both went inside.

I said, "What is this, Gallin? What's going on?"

Her eyes were on the doorway. She said quietly, "Shut up, Mason."

A moment later Silverman appeared in the doorway again, whistled and gestured to his boys to join him inside. The doors opened and three guys in jeans and leather jackets, all carrying assault rifles, climbed out and went inside. A hot stab of adrenaline pierced my gut.

"I don't like this. I'm going in there."

"Wait!" She put her hand on my arm. I turned to her and our eyes locked. She said, "We have the same instructions you have. Just take it easy."

A moment later Silverman emerged. Behind him were two of his boys and between them they had the colonel. Behind them was the third guy.

I opened the door and got out. They stopped and watched me approach. The colonel had a black eye, but aside from that he looked OK. I turned to Silverman.

"What's this bullshit you're pulling, Colonel? My instructions and yours are clear. You hand Colonel Cameron over to me and I take him back to DC. Hand him over."

His eyes traveled down to my feet and then up to my face again.

"I have my orders, Mr. Mason. I don't need you to

remind me. We are in Israel now, you have no jurisdiction here."

"I am not talking about jurisdiction, Colonel. I am talking about abiding by an agreement between our two governments."

He nodded a few times, like he wasn't in a hurry to stop nodding. Then he walked to his Land Rover and opened the rear passenger door. "I will hand Colonel Cameron over to you when we have finished a few administrative technicalities. Follow us."

They bundled Cameron in the back of the Land Rover and I returned to mine and Gallin's. As I climbed in and slammed the door I asked her, "Did you know about this?"

"No. I have no idea what's going on." She went to open the door, but Silverman climbed in and the truck took off into the dark. We went after them.

We drove through the dark for about ten minutes until we came to a main road. We crossed the road to a dirt track on the far side and started to climb steeply through a barren, rocky landscape peppered with gnarled bushes and boulders, until eventually we came to the mouth of a gully. It was a broad, triangular area of flat land bordered on two sides by steep hills, and on the third by a vertiginous drop into darkness.

Silverman's truck pulled over and stopped, and we pulled in behind it. I watched them all climb out and march Cameron to the front of the Land Rover, where the ground was flooded by the lights from the headlamps.

Gallin exploded, "This is bullshit!" and climbed out. I climbed out after and she marched over to where Silverman was standing.

"Would you mind telling me what the hell is going on, Colonel? My instructions were explicit. Collect Colonel Ian Cameron and ensure a seamless handover to the American agent Alex Mason, and escort them to the airport. You want to tell me how this charade fits in with your orders?"

His look would have frozen ice. "I would advise you to watch your tone with me, *Captain*."

"And I would advise you to watch your step with the people I represent, Colonel. You talk to me and you are talking to the director of the *Mossad Merkazi le-Modiin ule-Tafkidim Meyuhadim*. Now I am going to ask you one more time, what the hell do you think you are doing?"

SIXTEEN

HE GAVE HER THE ONCE-OVER, LIKE HE'D DONE TO me earlier. Then he walked over and stared Cameron in the face for a moment. Finally he turned and addressed me.

"Mr. Mason, we are allies, right? America and Israel. When the time came for us to return to the promised land, it was America who first recognized us as a state. And through our darkest, most difficult times, America has stood by us, as we have stood by America, friends and allies."

"So far, yes," I said with heavy irony.

He nodded his unhurried nod. "Have you any conception, have you any idea, at all, what would happen—not just to Israel but to the world, to the balance of power in the world, to the institutions of world democracy!—if the United States turned their back on Israel?"

It was a question that deserved some thought. So I thought about it for a moment before answering.

"Yes, I have some conception. The result would be catastrophic."

"More. More than catastrophic. We are looking at the possibility—no, the *probability* of a nuclear holocaust. If the United States withdraws its support from Israel, that signifies an *existential threat* to our nation and our people. Do you understand that? Can you imagine the *very existence* of the United States of America being under threat? It is a concept you cannot grasp, and yet it is a concept we live with, daily."

"I understand. At least intellectually, I understand."

He snorted something that was too bitter to be called a laugh. Then he pointed at Colonel Ian Cameron.

"This..." He licked his lips and looked up at the sky, like he was asking for help from some Old Testament god. "Me beliefs, my religion, my personal ideology, compel me to call him a man. But God knows I do not consider him even human! This *creature*, not content with enabling and facilitating the destruction of countless—*countless*—young lives; not content with mediating the relationship between General Mike Ustinov of the CIA and the Sinaloa Cartel, *not content* with encouraging and stimulating the war between the cartels and causing the murder of thousands of people in Mexico who need never have died—men, women, children, old and young alike—not content with all this, *Colonel Ian Cameron...*" He seemed to spit the words into the cold dust. "Organized, facilitated and enable the sale of rockets to Hezbollah, in the sure and certain knowledge that those rockets would be used against Israeli civilians."

A deadly silence fell. He watched me for a long moment, then turned and looked at Cameron. Cameron looked away, into the darkness.

Silverman took a couple of steps toward me. His voice had been rising in outrage, but now he spoke quietly.

"He organized, facilitated and enable the sale of rockets to Hezbollah, in the sure and certain knowledge that those rockets would be used against Israeli civilians, men, women and children, of all ages, from small babies, to the aged. Does he deny it?" He turned and looked at Cameron, and yelled, *"Do you deny it?"*

Cameron said nothing, and suddenly Silverman stormed to his Land Rover, wrenched open the door, reached inside and emerged with a copy of Cameron's book. He took it to the colonel and slammed it into the dust at his feet. Then turned to me with fury writ large in his eyes.

"He does not deny it, Mr. Mason! He *boasts* about it! He is the wild, devil may care, lovable Celtic rogue! The lovable rogue who enables the ruthless murder of thousands of innocent people! But that, Mr. Mason, is the tip of the iceberg."

He turned and looked at the colonel again. "Am I wrong, Colonel Cameron? You say nothing? You don't protest?" Silverman turned back to me. "It is the tip of the iceberg, Mr. Mason, because, directed by General Mike Ustinov, Colonel Ian Cameron systematically brought into his web of murder and corruption senators, governors, judges and law enforcement officers. There was collusion from the White House to the Mexican border and up to the border with Canada. And all for what? To secure oil concessions in Iran for friends of the administration." He pointed to the book lying in the dirt. "It is all in there. He boasts about it all in there. Now I am going to ask you another question. What lesson, what learning, do you think the ayatollahs in Iran will draw when their intelligence services read and analyze that book?"

I didn't answer and he yelled the question, red in the face and turning to bellow it a second time at Cameron.

"*What lesson will the ayatollahs in Iran draw when their intelligence services read and analyze that damned book? What lesson will they draw?*"

He turned to face me and stated quietly, "That the United States is no longer an unconditional ally of Israel. That the United States' loyalty to Israel as an ally is for sale, and can be bought with oil." He paused. "Mr. Mason, I am going to have to insist on an answer. Am I mistaken? Is that not the inference that the Ayatollahs must, perforce draw from that book?"

I took a deep breath and sighed. "Unless something were done to correct that impression, I would have to say you were right."

"Unless something were done to correct that impression." He walked back to Cameron and stared at him for a moment. Then he spoke. He raised his voice because he was speaking to me, though he was still staring at Cameron.

"Several discreet representations were made through confidential, diplomatic channels. The responses ranged from a defense of free speech which was noticeably muted when Salman Rushdie's fatwa was announced, to lectures on the free market and assurances that nobody could ever doubt the United States' robust defense of Israel's right to exist. But that was about it. The present administration, it seems," he turned now to face me, "has a taste for oil and a rather romantic perception of Islam."

I nodded. "OK, Colonel Silverman, you have made your

point, and I am sympathetic. But how is any of this going to help?"

He lifted his chin. "How is it going to help? I'll tell you. When we received the advance copy of the book and we analyzed its contents, we took a decision. We would target those people involved in the sale of missiles to Hezbollah, and we would execute them as a warning to the rest. Captain Gallin was given that mission and carried it out in an exemplary fashion. But Colonel Ian Cameron was to be brought to Israel and put on trial, for the world to see, and then executed. So that the White House, the Capitol, the Pentagon and Langley, as well as Tehran, would all see that though we love and support our friends, we need nobody and will not tolerate betrayal."

"But Colonel, my department—"

"Your department mediated an agreement between Washington and Israel. They will ensure that the guilty are punished, and they will take steps to shore up the relationship with Israel so that there is no risk from Tehran. Words. And in exchange for these words, I must hand this criminal over to you so that he can return to the United States and live as a millionaire on the proceeds from his book. The proceeds of his crimes."

I agree with you, Colonel. It sucks. Unfortunately that is the way of politics. A soldier has no greater enemy than his own politicians. But this, if you are planning what I think you are planning, is not the answer."

"What do you think I am planning, Mr. Mason?"

"A kangaroo court and an execution." He didn't say anything so I went on. "You asked me to think through the consequences of the publication of Colonel Cameron's book, and you were right. Now I am going to ask you to think through the consequences of such a trial. First you would discredit Israel as a democratic state governed by the rule of law. Then you would undermine the unity of Israel in the face of its enemies. And you know as well as I do that nothing is more important than unity when facing your enemy. And finally, you would have to kill an American government agent, because I can't stand by and let you do this."

Gallin spoke quietly at my side. "And an agent of the Mossad and a British citizen. You would do a lot more damage to Israel with this action than Cameron would with his book."

He turned away from me and walked up to Cameron. "You are guilty," he told him. "but God has decided to spare your life. When you get back to the USA, and you publish your filthy book, you will condemn, publicly, those who have betrayed America's friendship with Israel, and you will call on the government to right this wrong." He turned to me. "And you will advise your department that if the government's response is inadequate, they risk a nuclear holocaust in Iran." He paused long enough for me to offer him a skeptical frown. Then he said, "It was discussed in Cabinet, Mr. Mason. Make them understand: the perspective is very different here in Israel, from what it is in DC."

He took a key from his pocket and went to remove Cameron's handcuffs. One of the soldiers spoke up. He was young, in his twenties, clean shaven with very short dark hair. He said something in Hebrew and the colonel went very still. I glanced at Gallin.

"What's happening?"

"The lieutenant just told the colonel they are not prepared to let Cameron go. He has to be executed."

"Sweet Jesus..."

Silverman was answering the lieutenant. His voice was low and calm. But as he spoke the guy on Cameron's right, a big, older guy with black stubble and black eyes, put his rifle to Cameron's head.

Silverman raised his voice and pointed at me and Gallin. A sudden surge of anger made my belly hot. I muttered, "I've had enough of this," and walked up to Silverman and Cameron. Gallin was right behind me. I held my hand out to Silverman and said, "Give me the damned key." While he hesitated I scowled at the guy with the stubble. "Do you speak English?"

He answered me with hooded eyes. "I speak English."

"Then remove that weapon from this man's head, or I am going to take it and shove it up your ass. You are breaking the law and disobeying your commanding officer and your president. Now I am going to tell you what is going to happen here. I am going to take this man to my Land Rover, I am going to take him to the airport and I am going to return to the USA with him, as our two governments have agreed. Do you understand?"

I took hold of Cameron's arm and turned to Silverman. "Give me the damned key, will you?"

He reached out and dropped it in my hand, and a second later his head exploded. The explosion rocked me. I staggered and dragged Cameron to the ground with me. I heard a couple of shouts, saw Gallin hit the ground and half a second later saw the guy with the stubble aiming his rifle at me.

Gallin was on her feet, holding her Sig Sauer in both hands, pointing straight at Stubble's head. She bellowed, "All right! Freeze! That's enough! You have just murdered an IDF colonel! You are under arrest. Lay down your weapons!"

The young soldier who had shot the colonel swung his weapon on Gallin and a moment later the third guy, short and stocky with red hair, followed suit. I muttered to Cameron, "Stay down," and got slowly to my feet, looking Stubble in the eye and speaking as I went.

"We all need to start thinking here. One of you needs to be thinking that he just murdered his commanding officer. It does not get much worse than that, and you, pal, need to be thinking about how you mitigate that. Because right now you are guilty of treason. The other two of you need to be thinking, do you want to share in that guilt? Because as it stands, all three of you are guilty of this murder, and all three of you are guilty of treason. But come to your senses, and arrest the guy who just killed your colonel, and you might just get away with it."

The young guy's voice came shrill, "Commanding officer? He was a traitor! He was going to let that criminal go. We brought him here to stand trial before the American. And that is what we will do! Saul, we have heard the evidence and we have seen the proof. Do what you must do or I will do it for you, to your eternal shame!"

Saul must have been the guy with the stubble. Because he swallowed hard, looked at Gallin and then down at Cameron. Gallin spoke quietly.

"And what are you going to do then? You have murdered your colonel, then you murder an American that your government has agreed to return to America, and then?

Then will you kill a captain in the Mossad? And after that an American government agent? Where will you stop? You won't stop until you have destroyed Israel."

The redhead said, "He was a traitor, you are all traitors!"

I raised my voice. "You kill me and my department will come after you, Israel will lose the support of the Pentagon and the White House, the Mossad will come after you and your own government will make an example of you! Come to your senses for God's sake, and don't make it any worse."

Saul looked at the young lieutenant. "David, what should I do?"

"The four of them are found dead out here in the mountains. There is nothing to connect them to us. Shoot the bastard already!"

His eyes said he was going to do it. I exploded forward, using my right hand to thrust the cannon of his rifle up into the air. It exploded and I felt the heat of the shot burn into my hand, as I brought my left leg up to meet my right and delivered a thundering pendulum kick to his balls with my right instep. He let out an agonizing wheeze and let go of his weapon. I already had the cannon in my right. With my left I grabbed just behind the magazine and as my foot hit the ground I smashed the stock into his jaw.

For a moment time seemed to freeze. Ginger and the lieutenant both had their weapons trained on Gallin. Panic stirred in my gut and my chest. Whichever one I shot, the other would kill her. The stock slammed against my hip. My finger found the trigger and the weapon erupted as a hail of molten lead tore through the redhead's chest.

I didn't waste time. I turned my head, and saw the lieutenant's rifle spitting fire, but Gallin was not there. Again time seemed to freeze for a fraction of a second. Then a small black hole appeared between the lieutenant's eyes and the top of his head exploded in a fountain of red.

There was silence. I looked down and saw Gallin on one knee, with her Sig held out in front of her. I said, "Are you OK?"

She looked at me and laughed hysterically for maybe fifteen seconds. Then she stood and said, "Sorry. Yes, I'm OK. This was intense."

I nodded. "Intense, yes."

A movement behind me made me turn and look. Colonel Ian Cameron was standing. In his left hand he was holding the key to his cuffs. He was smiling, and in his right hand he had an automatic rifle.

"You dropped this," he said. "When you get back to the States, be sure to thank Uncle Sam for me." He laughed. "I really thought it was curtains there for a moment. You got some nice moves there, Mason." He tossed the key on the ground, leveled his weapon at us and started backing toward Silverman's Land Rover.

"I'm gonna say goodbye now, on account of I think I need to move to some climate that is better for my health. Somehow I think going back to the States with you ain't such a good idea." He gave another small laugh. "Oh! Foolish me! Did I ask you to thank Uncle Sam for me? 'Course you won't be able to, will ya? On account of being a little bit dead."

SEVENTEEN

I HURLED MYSELF AT GALLIN. HER HUNDRED AND twenty pounds never stood a chance against my two hundred and twenty. She went down and I landed on top of her as a hail of bullets tore over our heads. We would both have died, but somehow I managed to jump, collide and fall, and shoot all at the same time. My aim wasn't great, but I did manage to take out one of his headlamps. He clambered into the Land Rover and reversed at speed while Gallin screamed at me to get off her.

I did as she asked as the truck spun, right at the edge of the precipice, and hurtled away into the night. Gallin scrambled to her feet and ran after him. Then stopped and looked back at me, waving her hands in the air, taking them first to her forehead, then raising them up to implore God and finally dropping them in hopelessness toward the ground. Then repeating the whole process again while walking toward me, sagging and saying, "But...why...what...you..."

I put my arms around her and she rested her head on my chest. "You know what?" I said, "You're alive."

After a moment she put her arms around me and sighed. "I guess, but so is he."

"He won't get far. And besides, I'd rather be you alive than him dead..."

She pulled back a bit and frowned up at me. "That doesn't make any sense."

"Well, it kind of—"

"No. It doesn't. I mean, what does that mean? I would rather..."

"Gallin. I'm tired. It made sense to me at the time." I started walking toward her truck and she followed, holding her arms out wide again. "Of course you'd rather be alive than dead."

"You should take it as a compliment."

"You'd rather be *me?* What, are you a *woman* now?"

I climbed in and she got behind the wheel. "I mean it's obvious and impossible at the same time."

"Gallin, shut up."

"I'd rather be you alive than him dead. Jeez. *And* you let him get away."

She phoned the office and I phoned home. Nero said it was lamentable and her boss said we'd better come on down to Glilot and file a report. As it was, while she wrote and filed a report, I was interrogated for five hours. I go the impression Uncle Sam was not the flavor of the month down at the Mossad right then.

Finally, at about six in the morning, the door to the interrogation room opened and Gallin walked in. She had deep shadows under her eyes and her hair looked like she had a nest of nervous mice living in it. But she sighed and smiled, and that looked nice, and she held out her arm and said, "Come on, old friend, let's go get some coffee and some sleep."

We got a cab and told the driver to take us to the Tel Aviv Hilton, which was just five or ten minutes down the road. On the way I put my arm around her and she rested her head on my shoulder and closed her eyes. I thought for a moment and said, "What are your plans? Are you going back to London? Or do you have to stay here?"

"No plans," she said sleepily. "According to the chief, my job is done. Colonel Cameron has effectively been pardoned, and if he wants to make his way back to the USA under his own steam, he is welcome. I'm taking a couple of weeks to recover. I am bushed."

"I have the company jet here."

She snorted and shook her head. "Company jet..."

"Why don't you come back with me. I need a break too. We'll go somewhere and eat oysters."

"That sounds like a plan, Mr. Mason."

A vague sense of disquiet made me look out the rear window, but there was nothing to see.

The hotel was still and quiet. The receptionist wished us a good morning and we went up to my room. While she showered I ordered eggs, bacon, croissants and lots of coffee, and while she lay on the bed I showered. By the time I was done the breakfast had arrived. We stuffed our faces and then slept like the dead for four hours straight.

———

AND WHILE WE slept like the dead, in a narrow alley between Yehuda Margoza Street and Rabi Khanina Street, in a small, shabby room behind a dilapidated door in a seedy building, Colonel Ian Cameron made a phone call on Colonel Silverman's cell.

"Joaquin, how you doin', pal?"

"Who is this...?"

"It's me, Ian Cameron, remember me?" He could hear a party in the background. "You havin' a fiesta, amigo?"

"Ian? I thought you were dead? You know what has happened here? We havin' a meetin' right now, to see who takes over, and how we gonna punish these bastards."

"That's good news, Joaquin. The crown should go to you, pal. A lot of people would like me to be dead, Joaquin, and believe it or not, that is what all of this was about. I'll fill you in when we meet, meantime, let me tell you something. I just killed four Mossad agents—"

"*Mossad?* Are you kidding me?"

"No, I am deadly serious. It's a long story. But the upshot is, I can give you the name, and the location, of the bitch who murdered Francisco and Ismael."

"Bitch? It was a woman?"

"Yeah, and I can lead you right to her and her partner. I just have two favors to ask you."

"Anything, tell me."

"I need you to get me out of Tel Aviv, and when the time comes, I want to kill the bitch with my own hands."

"You got it, my friend. Give me your address and I will have you out of there in twenty-four hours."

"Oh, and Joaquin? Get me some money, will you?"

He had waited all night at the Glilot Interchange, on the

corner of Namir Road. It had been a risk to spend the night in a parked Land Rover that close to the Mossad Headquarters. But he figured it was worth it. And it had been. Just after dawn he had seen them come out and climb into a cab. And the big prize had come when he'd seen the cab take them both to Mason's hotel. He'd had a hunch, but seeing them both go into the hotel, and ride the elevator up to his room together, had been all the confirmation he had needed. And he'd got some good pictures of them doing it.

He'd figured he had a few hours so he had breakfast at the hotel, keeping his eye on the elevators. Then he'd gone out and took a cab back to old Jaffa.

Now he showered and dressed and went out for a stroll along Yefet Street, north toward the beach and the Hilton, just over two miles away. After about half an hour, when he was standing looking out at the sea on the Homat Hayam Promenade, his cell rang.

He checked the screen before answering.

"Yeah?"

"Where are you?"

"I'm on the corner of Nahum Goldman Street and Homat Hayam Promenade, on the beach, looking at the sea. There's a bar by the parking lot. I'm sitting on a big rock."

"OK, stay there. A friend is gonna come and see you. He's got something for you. You tell him where the bitch is."

"That's great, Joaquin, but I want this understood: I make the kill."

"That's understood."

He sat, wishing he had a Camel to smoke, and watched the small waves roll in and break on the shore. He closed his eyes and reflected that it was impossible to hear the sound of waves without seeing them in your imagination. Impossible to feel the cool, damp sand of a beach at night, without hearing the waves. Maybe all the senses were connected somehow, sight, hearing, taste, smell and touch.

Touch.

Touch was the sense that gave life, and extinguished it.

He opened his eyes and turned them back to the ocean. He wondered vaguely why he felt no regret. Colonel Silverman's speech that night had moved him. It had been a good speech. But however hard he searched inside he could find no remorse, no regret, and the notion of guilt made him laugh. The only feeling he had that carried any power at all was the rage he felt against the woman called Gallin. He wanted to make her suffer, make her beg, and when she was pleading he was going to enjoy killing her.

He wondered if that made him a sociopath, but dismissed the notion as absurd. What he was, was a normal, healthy man in a world that had become weak and flaccid from having everything given to them on a plate.

He saw a dark BMW roll into the parking lot and pull up twenty yards away. A guy in an expensive Italian suit climbed out and stood looking around. He spotted the colonel sitting on the big rock and walked toward him. He had greased hair and dark skin, and shades that had probably cost him a thousand bucks.

He stopped in front of the colonel and smiled. "Excuse me, I am supposed to meet somebody here. A Colonel Ian Cameron?"

The colonel stood and shook the guy's hand. "That's me."

"I am Diego Romero." He pointed to the bar. "Shall we have a drink?"

"If you're paying. I am broke."

The man gave an urbane laugh. "My friend, by the time you have finished your drink, you will no longer be broke!"

The colonel smiled. "That's two nice things you've said in less than a minute. Let's go."

They sat at a table under a white parasol. Romero ordered a mango juice and the colonel ordered a Scotch and soda. While they were waiting Romero pulled a fat manila envelope from his pocket and handed it across the table. "This is ten thousand dollars and a thousand dollars in shekels. Now, I think you have some information for me?"

The colonel stuffed the envelope in his pocket and gave Romero the kind of smile a snake might give a cornered mouse.

"I have information for you. But first I am going to tell you something I have told Joaquin twice already. So this will be the third time. I am going to take you to the woman who killed Francisco Gallardo, and Ismael Zamora. And I will be grateful for any help you can give me. But she is mine. I execute the sentence. I hope that is understood."

"Perfectly. What do you need?"

"They are either going to stay in Israel, or they are going to go to London or DC. So I need them watched while I get a shower, some food and sleep and some new clothes."

"Done, where are they?"

"They are at the Hilton. Give me your number and I'll send you some pictures so you can identify them."

When Romero had received the pictures he sent them to Joaquin Sanchez Martin in Mexico, and to a couple of guys in Tel Aviv. When he was done the colonel told him, "Now, when they leave, I want to know where they go, and I want them met at the other end and followed. I want to know if they go to her house, to his house, to a hotel..." He spread his hands. "Wherever they go, when I arrive, I want to be taken to their door."

Romero nodded. "As we speak there are a couple of boys on their way to the Hilton. None of what you ask is gonna be a problem, Colonel. We want this bitch real bad. You cannot just go and kill the head of Sinaloa, and walk away. The very least it is gonna cost is your life. That is the minimum. So we gonna help you in every way we can. There is one thing Joaquin is askin' for. He wants to see the pictures. He wants the bitch decapitated, and he wants a picture of that."

The colonel chuckled. "Damned barbarian. Sure, it's the least I can do. Maybe I'll send him her head in the diplomatic pouch, via Bill Ortega. Tell him I said that."

Romero looked out at the bright sea for a moment. When he turned back to the colonel he shifted his sunglasses to the top of his head, like it was a form of respect.

"Bill Ortega is dead. Was he a good friend of yours?"

The colonel shrugged. "I had two good friends, Ismael Zamora and Francisco Gallardo. What happened to Bill?"

Romero held up the phone and showed him one of the pictures the colonel had sent him. "He took this man to see Ismael, at Joaquin's villa. He was looking for you. The next day this woman killed him. Joaquin made an example of Bill."

"You don't say. Bill took Mason to see Ismael?" He snorted. "Asshole."

"OK, I got some things to do. I drop you at my place, you have a shower and something to eat. Get some sleep. As soon as they move I let you know."

"You're a gentleman, Diego. I won't forget your help."

Romero dropped some money on the table and they left the bar.

———

A LITTLE OVER two miles to the north, as the crow flies, Gallin sat up, yawned and stretched. She walked unsteadily to the bathroom, stripped off her clothes and stood under the shower, switching from hot to cold and back again.

I had been awake for a while, staring at the ceiling. I was exhausted, but in her sleep she had rolled over and put her head on my shoulder, and after that I couldn't sleep. I could hear the shower going in the bathroom. I sat up and stared at the floor for a while, then, wondering what the hell I was doing, I called out, "*You need any help?*"

She didn't answer for a moment and I thanked the Lord she hadn't heard me. Then she called back, "*Yeah, you could do my back! I can't reach!*"

I shook my head at my feet and said quietly to myself, "You do not want to do this. This is a *bad* idea..." Then I stood, and stood staring at the bathroom door, which was open ajar. "This is a *really* bad idea, Mason. But you just know you are going to do it..."

"*You coming or not?*"

"*Yeah! Coming!*"

I stood in the doorway, leaning on the jamb. I could see her form through the frosted glass. She had her back to me.

There was a furnace building up heat in my belly and I managed to control my voice enough to say, "Where's the soap?"

Her hand appeared through the sliding door holding a plastic bottle. "It's gel," she said.

Then there was a knock on the door. I said, "Hang on," closed the bathroom and opened the door. There was a guy there with oiled hair and an expensive Italian suit. He looked Hispanic and if we'd been on the American continent I would have said he had cartel written all over him. When he spoke his accent was Mexican.

"Bobby? I'm lookin' for Bobby Cohen?"

I shook my head. "Sorry, you must have the wrong room."

He looked at the door, laughed and rolled his eyes. "Wrong room, and wrong floor! Sorry to have disturbed you. You have a great day."

I closed the door and stood staring at my hand on the wood. I turned and saw Gallin wrapped in a bath towel, drying her hair. "I got tired of waiting," she said. "What is it?"

"I think we have a problem. I think the colonel got busy on the phone."

EIGHTEEN

WE WENT DOWN TO THE LOBBY AND I SETTLED THE
bill while Gallin had the Land Rover sent up. I stepped out.
I had no luggage or hand baggage. If we were going to try
and lose a tail, I didn't want to send the message that we
were headed for the airport. I scanned the area for anything
or anyone who looked wrong, but didn't see anything. So I
climbed in the passenger seat.

We pulled out of the hotel and onto Arlozorov Street,
and nobody tried to shoot us or follow us. There was a lot of
traffic, so it was hard to tell if anyone was with us, but when
Gallin turned into Itzik Manger, I noticed a dark Audi
turned with us. I said, "The Audi."

"I got it."

She took Be'er Tuvya, Metsada and Yodfat in rapid
succession. The Audi stayed with us. Then she turned into
Dizengoff and almost immediately onto Arlozorov, right
where we had started, and he was right behind us. He knew
he was blown and he'd given up trying.

I said, "We have a problem. Cameron has called in the cavalry. And this guy doesn't care that we've seen him."

She glanced in the mirror and smiled. It was a disturbing smile. "Problem? No problem, Alex."

She swung the wheel sharply and took a sudden right. I didn't see the name but it didn't matter because a moment later she had fishtailed left and right again and suddenly we were surging onto the Ayalon Highway. She had four lanes to play with and she opened up the big V8 and we thundered forward. For a moment I thought maybe we had lost him, but when I looked back I could see him weaving through the traffic, trying to close on us.

"If you can pull ahead a little more and come off the highway we might lose him long enough to make the airport."

She smiled at me and sighed. It was an odd, affectionate sigh. "Oh, Alex," she said, and began to slow.

At the Kiryat Ganim interchange she veered east onto Highway 431. The Audi was closing, but not fast. And at Azarya she turned south again onto Highway 6. Here she opened up again and pushed the truck to a hundred and twenty miles per hour. We hurtled south through lush, cultivated fields, weaving easily from lane to lane. And all the while the Audi stayed with us.

At the Qiryat Gat interchange the landscape began to change. At first there were woodlands, interspersed with rolling green pastures, but by the time we had started to climb toward Hura, the rolling green hills started to give way to rocky hills, shrubs and gray chalky earth.

Just outside Hura she spun the wheel and fishtailed into a sharp left and for a moment I thought we were going to roll. The tires screamed on the blacktop, and just as we tipped she hit the gas and we surged forward. Behind us was the Audi. Ahead of us was a narrow country road that wound its way through dry, arid fields and scattered houses. She rocketed forward and must have hit a hundred over the mile, then crashed down through the gears, sending the revs screaming to seven thousand, before she braked and spun the wheel right to lurch and bounce onto a dirt track that wound up into the hills.

The Audi made the turn, but bounced and jarred painfully when it hit the track. Now he had to slow while we pulled ahead, leaving a billowing fog of dust behind us.

"Where are we going?" I asked.

She grinned, then gurgled. "Nowhere," she said, "to the airport."

She came as close as you can get to a handbrake turn without a handbrake, stopped and revved the engine while we sat and watched the billowing cloud of dust drift toward us. After a moment the Audi's automatic fog lights appeared through the cloud. She put the truck in drive and I exploded, "*Jesus!*" as I realized what she was going to do.

She screamed, "*Brace!*" as she hurled the truck forward across the road to smash into the front passenger door and send the car screaming into the side of the road.

I had the door open before we had stopped and I swung down and ran. Gallin was out the other side with a Sig Sauer in her hand. The doors of the Audi were opening. The front passenger was the first to get out. He was in a bad way, bleeding profusely from a gash to his head. I pulled the P226 from under my arm and yelled, "*Freeze! Get on the ground!*"

That obviously didn't seem like a good idea to him

because instead of freezing and getting on the ground he pulled a Glock from behind his back. I double tapped him in the chest and he staggered and folded onto the road.

Meanwhile Gallin had opened the driver's door and dragged out the driver. I was approaching the rear doors and saw him pull a knife from his back pocket. I yelled, "*Knife!*" and she slammed the car door in his face and put two rounds through his head.

That was when the windshield exploded, shattered by automatic fire. I saw Gallin drop. But before I could do anything the rear door opened and a guy with an Italian suit and a ponytail lunged out, waving a semi-automatic at me. It exploded and I felt the hot rush of molten lead brush past my face. A second shot would have torn through my chest if I hadn't jumped to my left. His third shot was wild because I had closed in and grabbed his wrist in my left hand, thrust the Sig into his floating ribs and emptied four shots into his liver. He dropped to the dirt and I put a fifth between his eyes for good measure.

All of that had taken no more than three or four seconds, but all that while I had been hearing the roar of an assault rifle and the ping and whine of slugs ricocheting off metal and rocks.

I looked for Gallin and saw her sprawled at the front of the Audi. In a split second I realized whoever it was could not see her, but could see me, and I ran with winged feet for the trunk. As I got there he was getting out and ramming a magazine into a Heckler and Koch 416. He put it to his shoulder, aiming right at me, and a quiet, calm voice in my head said, "Oh, so this is how it happens." I raised the Sig and took aim at his head. He screamed, "*Where's the bitch?*"

And as I went to squeeze the trigger, he was suddenly striding behind the car toward the hood. I couldn't get a bead so I ran, yelling at him, "*Hey! Asshole! I'm here! What's the matter with you?*" I pulled off a round but he was moving too erratically and the shot went wide.

He glanced at me. His face was twisted with rage. He screamed, "*Where is she?*"

I had an impossible choice. Take two steps to my right and hope to lead him away from her, and be unable to protect her if he found her, or take two steps to my left, where I could protect her, but lead him straight to her.

I did the only thing I could. I kept my gun trained on him and walked to where she was hunkered down on the road. I stood over her and looked him in the eye.

"Drop your weapon, Colonel. You blew it. It's over. Look at her—just look at her—and I will blow your brains right out of your head."

He smiled at me. "You asshole," he said, and trained his weapon on Gallin. Because his head was tilted forward, the 9mm round punched through the top of his head and exited though his spine at the base of his skull. So any message his brain had sent to his trigger finger, never got delivered.

Gallin had fired at the same instant and her round had punched through his forehead, hit my round, fused with it and driven it out through his spine, at the base of his skull. The forensic team would later find the two, fused bullets and send them as a memento to Gallin, who would give them to me on my birthday, the following month. But that is a whole different story.

Right then I helped her to her feet and we walked the few steps back to the Land Rover, where I told her, "You are clean out of your mind. Insane is sane compared to you. You are…" I shook my head. She smiled. "You're lost for words, right?"

"Yes."

"That's nice."

I frowned at her and looked back at the carnage in and around the smoldering Audi. I sighed and gave up. "Are you OK?"

"Yes, thanks for asking. How are you?"

I nodded, shrugged, spread my hands and made other displays of despair. "Oh, I'm fine, thanks. Do you come here often?"

She started laughing, a kind of helpless laughter that comes with the release of intense emotion. After a moment it became contagious and I started to laugh too, wondering if her insanity had become contagious as well. She came to me and put her arms around me and we stood like that for a while, helpless with laughter, until eventually it subsided, and we both climbed into the Land Rover and drove away.

As we cruised gently back toward Tel Aviv, she made a phone call in which she spoke a lot in Hebrew, and didn't give the guy at the other end the chance to get a word in edgeways, though I did hear him say, *"OK! OK! OK!"* at the end, like he couldn't take it anymore.

When she was done I called Nero. Lovelock's sinful dark chocolate voice put me through and the gargantuan gaffer said, "Alex—"

"Sir, Colonel Ian Cameron decided that he did not want to come with me to DC."

"Why?"

"Because he though we were going to prosecute him. He

had decided that he wanted to disappear into South America and live there on the proceeds of his book, and party with his friends from Sinaloa."

"I am surprised he had any left."

"Indeed," I said, and thought for a moment I was beginning to talk like him. "Well, he did have some left and a few of them were in Tel Aviv. So, while Captain Gallin and I were on our way to the airport, they ambushed us and we killed them."

"They ambushed you, and you killed them."

"Yes, sir. It was touch and go."

"So I understand that Colonel Cameron is no longer with us."

"He may well be on his way to the Hall of the Fallen, sir, in the arms of a Valkyrie."

"Your facetiousness is relentless, Alex."

"Yes, sir."

"Are you on your way back to Washington?"

"Yes, sir. That other Valkyrie is waiting for us at the Tel Aviv airport. I am going to take a couple of weeks' holiday, sir, and Captain Gallin and I are going to eat oysters in New England somewhere, and attend to some unfinished business."

"Fine. Let me know when you have recovered your senses."

"Yes sir."

"Are you on your way back to Washington?"

I hung up and we drive in silence for a while. Then Gallin said, "Unfinished business?"

I nodded. "Your back. I never got to scrub it."

"Bah!" she said. "You're still thinking about that? I managed. I am pretty flexible, you know."

"Sure, but a promise is a promise."

"I don't remember you promising. You just said, 'Yeah, coming.'"

I looked out of the window, at the gray earth and the shrubs sliding by.

"You didn't hear," I said to the window, "because of the powerful hiss of the water, but I actually said, 'Yeah, I promise to wash your back, I'm coming.'"

"Bull—"

"It's the truth—"

"Bull—"

"Truth—"

And so we rolled peacefully on through the afternoon, to the waiting Valkyrie.

EPILOGUE

Alasdair Cameron sat in his favorite chair beside the fire, smoking his pipe and sipping his best single malt. He was watching the news. A woman in a khaki shirt and a ponytail was standing out in some remote part of the Israeli countryside. Behind her there was a mangled car, an ambulance and several police cars, all with flashing red and blue lights. Men and women in uniform, with reflective yellow vests, were picking through the shattered glass, inspecting the area. The woman, whose name was Penny, was talking to the camera.

"I have to tell you, David, that the details are very sketchy, and the authorities here in Israel are saying very little at the moment. However, what I am hearing unofficially is that Colonel Ian Cameron, who disappeared just a couple of days ago somewhere between 59th Street and Fifth Avenue, in Manhattan, after giving a talk at his book launch, was among the dead. He appears to have been shot twice in the head. There is speculation that he was executed because of the content of his book, due to be launched next month, *Sex Drugs and Rock 'n' Roll at the White House*. Though, as I say, that is just speculation at this stage.

"It is also interesting to note that the three other men found dead at the scene were all Mexican nationals, and all were gunned down in what appears to have been an ambush. That is all we have right now, but as details become available I'll keep you updated."

Alasdair reached for his cell phone and dialed a number. Araminta was at her office and grabbed the phone without looking at the screen.

"Good evening, Araminta. How are you? Do you happen to be watching the news?"

"Alasdair, what a surprise. No, should I be?"

"Yes. They've found Ian."

"Oh, thank God! Where is he? Is he all right?"

"Well, now. I think, Araminta, or may I call you Mini now? I think I just became your new best friend. They found him on a country road in Israel. Him, his car and his three pals from Sinaloa had all been shot to pieces."

"Oh, no. Oh, I am so sorry to hear that. I was really fond of Ian."

"He was a ruthless, heartless, sociopathic son of a bitch. But now I am his heir and sole beneficiary of his estate, and that makes all the rights to his book mine."

"Yes—"

"Arrange a few talks and interviews for me, and this is going to drive sales through the roof. I can tell you some stories about Ian, oh boy can I..."

In his study, unheard by Alasdair who was talking to

Araminta about his dead brother, the news continued in the background. The anchor was saying:

"In other news, Senator Walther Gannett, who had been active on several National Security Committees, was found this morning hanged in his study. The coroner has recorded the cause of death as suicide, based on a handwritten note which the senator left on his desk. He claimed in the note that the upcoming publication of Colonel Ian Cameron's book, *Sex Drugs and Rock 'n' Roll at the White House*, would ruin his reputation and his career, and left him no option but to take his own life.

"The book, which, based on advanced sales, is due to top the *New York Times* best seller list a full month before it is due to be published, has been causing quite a stir nationwide. In California, Supreme Court Judge Judith Obregon took the unprecedented step of resigning, citing the book as the cause, and has allegedly turned state's evidence..."

And all across the United States, anxious, frightened men and women watched the news unfold on their television screens, while slowly, mile by mile, men, cruel, violent men, moved north from Sinaloa, with murder and vengeance on their minds.

Don't miss FLASHPOINT. The riveting sequel in the Alex Mason Thriller series.

Scan the QR code below to purchase FLASHPOINT.

Or go to: righthouse.com/flashpoint

NOTE: flip to the very end to read an exclusive sneak peak...

DON'T MISS ANYTHING!

If you want to stay up to date on all new releases in this series, with these authors, or with any of our new deals, you can do so by joining our newsletters below.

In addition, you will immediately gain access to our entire *Right House VIP Library,* which currently includes *ORIGINS*—a full length prequel novel to *ODIN*.

righthouse.com/email

(Easy to unsubscribe. No spam. Ever.)

ALSO BY DAVID ARCHER

Up to date books can be found at:
www.righthouse.com/david-archer

ROGUE THRILLERS
Gates of Hell (Book 1)
Hell's Fury (Book 2)

JACOB HUNTER THRILLERS
The Kyiv File (Book 1)
The Bogota File (Book 2)

PETER BLACK THRILLERS
Burden of the Assassin (Book 1)
The Man Without A Face (Book 2)
Unpunished Deeds (Book 3)
Hunter Killer (Book 4)
Silent Shadows (Book 5)
The Last Run (Book 6)
Dark Corners (Book 7)
Ghost Operative (Book 8)

ALEX MASON THRILLERS
Odin (Book 1)
Ice Cold Spy (Book 2)
Mason's Law (Book 3)
Assets and Liabilities (Book 4)
Russian Roulette (Book 5)

Executive Order (Book 6)
Dead Man Talking (Book 7)
All The King's Men (Book 8)
Flashpoint (Book 9)
Brotherhood of the Goat (Book 10)
Dead Hot (Book 11)
Blood on Megiddo (Book 12)
Son of Hell (Book 13)

NOAH WOLF THRILLERS
Code Name Camelot (Book 1)
Lone Wolf (Book 2)
In Sheep's Clothing (Book 3)
Hit for Hire (Book 4)
The Wolf's Bite (Book 5)
Black Sheep (Book 6)
Balance of Power (Book 7)
Time to Hunt (Book 8)
Red Square (Book 9)
Highest Order (Book 10)
Edge of Anarchy (Book 11)
Unknown Evil (Book 12)
Black Harvest (Book 13)
World Order (Book 14)
Caged Animal (Book 15)
Deep Allegiance (Book 16)
Pack Leader (Book 17)
High Treason (Book 18)
A Wolf Among Men (Book 19)
Rogue Intelligence (Book 20)
Alpha (Book 21)

Rogue Wolf (Book 22)
Shadows of Allegiance (Book 23)
In the Grip of Darkness (Book 24)

SAM PRICHARD MYSTERIES
The Grave Man (Book 1)
Death Sung Softly (Book 2)
Love and War (Book 3)
Framed (Book 4)
The Kill List (Book 5)
Drifter: Part One (Book 6)
Drifter: Part Two (Book 7)
Drifter: Part Three (Book 8)
The Last Song (Book 9)
Ghost (Book 10)
Hidden Agenda (Book 11)

SAM AND INDIE MYSTERIES
Aces and Eights (Book 1)
Fact or Fiction (Book 2)
Close to Home (Book 3)
Brave New World (Book 4)
Innocent Conspiracy (Book 5)
Unfinished Business (Book 6)
Live Bait (Book 7)
Alter Ego (Book 8)
More Than It Seems (Book 9)
Moving On (Book 10)
Worst Nightmare (Book 11)
Chasing Ghosts (Book 12)
Serial Superstition (Book 13)

CHANCE REDDICK THRILLERS
Innocent Injustice (Book 1)
Angel of Justice (Book 2)
High Stakes Hunting (Book 3)
Personal Asset (Book 4)

CASSIE MCGRAW MYSTERIES
What Lies Beneath (Book 1)
Can't Fight Fate (Book 2)
One Last Game (Book 3)
Never Really Gone (Book 4)

ALSO BY BLAKE BANNER

Up to date books can be found at:
www.righthouse.com/blake-banner

ROGUE THRILLERS
Gates of Hell (Book 1)
Hell's Fury (Book 2)

ALEX MASON THRILLERS
Odin (Book 1)
Ice Cold Spy (Book 2)
Mason's Law (Book 3)
Assets and Liabilities (Book 4)
Russian Roulette (Book 5)
Executive Order (Book 6)
Dead Man Talking (Book 7)
All The King's Men (Book 8)
Flashpoint (Book 9)
Brotherhood of the Goat (Book 10)
Dead Hot (Book 11)
Blood on Megiddo (Book 12)
Son of Hell (Book 13)

HARRY BAUER THRILLER SERIES
Dead of Night (Book 1)
Dying Breath (Book 2)
The Einstaat Brief (Book 3)

Quantum Kill (Book 4)
Immortal Hate (Book 5)
The Silent Blade (Book 6)
LA: Wild Justice (Book 7)
Breath of Hell (Book 8)
Invisible Evil (Book 9)
The Shadow of Ukupacha (Book 10)
Sweet Razor Cut (Book 11)
Blood of the Innocent (Book 12)
Blood on Balthazar (Book 13)
Simple Kill (Book 14)
Riding The Devil (Book 15)
The Unavenged (Book 16)
The Devil's Vengeance (Book 17)
Bloody Retribution (Book 18)
Rogue Kill (Book 19)
Blood for Blood (Book 20)

DEAD COLD MYSTERY SERIES
An Ace and a Pair (Book 1)
Two Bare Arms (Book 2)
Garden of the Damned (Book 3)
Let Us Prey (Book 4)
The Sins of the Father (Book 5)
Strange and Sinister Path (Book 6)
The Heart to Kill (Book 7)
Unnatural Murder (Book 8)
Fire from Heaven (Book 9)
To Kill Upon A Kiss (Book 10)
Murder Most Scottish (Book 11)

The Butcher of Whitechapel (Book 12)
Little Dead Riding Hood (Book 13)
Trick or Treat (Book 14)
Blood Into Wine (Book 15)
Jack In The Box (Book 16)
The Fall Moon (Book 17)
Blood In Babylon (Book 18)
Death In Dexter (Book 19)
Mustang Sally (Book 20)
A Christmas Killing (Book 21)
Mommy's Little Killer (Book 22)
Bleed Out (Book 23)
Dead and Buried (Book 24)
In Hot Blood (Book 25)
Fallen Angels (Book 26)
Knife Edge (Book 27)
Along Came A Spider (Book 28)
Cold Blood (Book 29)
Curtain Call (Book 30)

THE OMEGA SERIES
Dawn of the Hunter (Book 1)
Double Edged Blade (Book 2)
The Storm (Book 3)
The Hand of War (Book 4)
A Harvest of Blood (Book 5)
To Rule in Hell (Book 6)
Kill: One (Book 7)
Powder Burn (Book 8)
Kill: Two (Book 9)
Unleashed (Book 10)

The Omicron Kill (Book 11)
9mm Justice (Book 12)
Kill: Four (Book 13)
Death In Freedom (Book 14)
Endgame (Book 15)

ABOUT US

Right House is an independent publisher created by authors for readers. We specialize in Action, Thriller, Mystery, and Crime novels.

If you enjoyed this novel, then there is a good chance you will like what else we have to offer! Please stay up to date by using any of the links below.

Join our mailing lists to stay up to date -->
righthouse.com/email
Visit our website --> righthouse.com
Contact us --> contact@righthouse.com

 facebook.com/righthousebooks

 x.com/righthousebooks

instagram.com/righthousebooks

EXCLUSIVE SNEAK PEAK OF...

FLASHPOINT

PROLOGUE

THE HEAT WAS HEAVY UNDER A MOLTEN SUN. IT didn't sparkle on the Atlantic Ocean. It lay like an incandescent sheet of steel, blinding to look at and obscuring the waves beneath its glare, in the Gulf of Cadiz. A group of men stood clustered around an apparently haphazard collection of machines. Some were mounted on trucks, Land Rovers and Jeeps. Others were set on the ground and had cables, like tendrils, stretching out across the wild scrubland of the Coto Doñana nature reserve. Along the cables were sensors that probed deep into the ground beneath the nature reserve, deep into the very bowels of the Earth.

The technology was cutting edge, more advanced than anything in Europe or the States. It was the result of millions of dollars of investment in research and development in particle physics resonance; and it had been developed specifically for this one job: to find crude oil deposits deep underground in Andalusia, in the south of Spain.

And it had been developed, in absolute secrecy, by

Russian laboratories subcontracted to the Russian Department of Advanced Research, which was in turn a sub-department of the Office for Innovative Design and Development, a branch of the top-secret Russian Research Institute at Tver.

It was one of several projects stretching across the autonomous region of Andalusia, from the deserts of Almeria and Granada in the east, through the sedimentary rock formations of the mountains of Malaga and eastern Cadiz, right across to the flats of the Atlantic coast of Cadiz and Huelva.

Dr. Jose Carlos Montilla was the head of the project. He had the data in from Almeria and Granada, he had just received the data from the mountains of Malaga, and now he was reading the data coming back from the sensors across the coast of Cadiz and Huelva. As he read it he sent it to print and ran across the flats back toward his field office. His belly was on fire and his head was reeling.

He burst through the cabin door. His assistant was at the computer and looked around as he came in. He snapped, "Out! Go! Go!"

She scuttled out and he slammed the door, sat and picked up the telephone that gave him a secure line to the office of Benjamin Musa in Seville, at his office in the Palace of San Telmo, the seat of the Junta de Andalucia, the Andalusian autonomous executive. Benjamin Musa was a powerful man. He was the head of the Andalusian Socialist Party and the leader of the opposition. He had risen to his position of power through a subtle use of bribery, and where that had failed, blackmail. He owned Montilla both because he had proof of the latter's use of drugs—which he himself had provided for him—and because he now provided him with a thousand euros a month as a supplement to his salary; a thousand euros on which Montilla had become completely dependent.

Musa snatched up the telephone.

"Yes!"

"Benjamin, I have all the data in. You will not believe this. Are you alone?"

"Yes. Tell me."

"There are deep oil reserves running from beneath the Mediterranean coast of Almeria right across Andalusia and out into the Gulf of Cadiz. As far as I can tell it reaches out into the Alboran Sea. It is *vast*. I have never seen anything like it."

Benjamin Musa laughed. "Oh, that is good, Jose Carlos, that is very good. I need your report on my desk by this evening. Absolutely *nobody* must get this information but me. Get on it now, not a word to anyone."

Jose Carlos hesitated. "Benjamin, I have done what you wanted. You will now release me?"

"Yes, Jose Carlos, of course I will. A promise is a promise. But let's not waste time. Put that report together and get it to me before six PM. And you will be a free man."

Benjamin Musa put down the phone and sat a moment gazing at the bright sunshine beyond his triple-glazed window. He watched the giant pine tree by the river on the Paseo de las Delicias, swaying in total silence. He looked at the London plane trees on the Paseo de Roma. He smiled. Achieving this corner office had been a triumph. What he was going to do now would dwarf anything he had achieved in the past.

He opened a drawer and extracted the secure, dedicated phone he had there, and dialed a number in Moscow. And two thousand five hundred miles away, to the north and east, Colonel Alexandrina Vitsin picked up her receiver and took her time putting it to her ear, as she exhaled smoke through her nose.

"Yes, Musa."

"The results are in. The report will be on my desk by six this evening, eight PM your time."

"Good. What steps will you take?"

"I will make a statement outside the Parliament here in Seville—"

"No."

She could almost hear him frown. "No?"

"Madrid. Palacio de la Cortes, on the steps of your parliament. Alert the press that you plan to make a statement. CNN, BBC, Reuters, everybody. Next week."

He nodded. "Yes, yes OK. I'll let you know when it's arranged."

She didn't answer. She hung up.

Benjamin Musa sat looking at the phone for a moment, chewing his lip. He had never met the colonel, but he had a mental image of what she looked like. He had often fantasized about slapping her violently. Now he sighed and put the thought aside. He dialed another number, in Seville. It rang twice and a raw voice made rough by unfiltered cigarettes and cognac said, "What?"

"Tonight. Steal a car. Make it look like a hit and run, or a mugging..."

"Don't tell me how to do my job. The price went up." A

cruel smile in the voice. "I know how important this is to you."

"How much?"

"Twenty K."

Quique was a gypsy. He was the one guy he had never been able to blackmail. Gypsies were all about family and closing ranks, honor and pride. If he had Quique killed, he would soon follow him to the grave. And if he stopped using him, they would destroy him. He would have to deal with them sooner or later. But not yet.

"OK, twenty thousand, but Quique?"

"What is it, Benny?"

"Don't push too far. Even you have a limit."

"Sure, you just tell me when I get there."

His laugh was like sawing wood. Musa hung up and looked at the silent, waving trees again. By six he would have his report, by ten the loose end of Jose Carlos would be tied up; and early next week he would light the fuse under the biggest crisis Europe had seen since Hitler invaded Poland on September 3rd, 1939.

CHAPTER 1

On Tuesday, 5ᵀᴴ September, at ten o'clock in the morning, the camera crews, photographers and reporters began to gather on the sidewalk outside the Congress on the Plaza de los Palacios. There were three police riot vans placed strategically around the square. Thirteen steps rose from the sidewalk to the six Greco-Roman columns that held the Palladian portico. At the top, in front of the massive oak doors two cops in balaclavas stood with assault rifles. The doors were open and four more armed guards stood inside.

By ten thirty the sidewalk was jammed with people. Several news anchors were speaking to cameras, while crowds gathered either side of the road, waiting to see what was going to happen. The CNN anchor was saying, "Madrid is rife with gossip, but it seems nobody knows for sure, Alysin, what is going to happen today. Benjamin Musa, the controversial leader of the Andalusian Socialist Party, leader of the opposition in the autonomous community of Andalusia, has stated that he will make a statement to the nation here, on the steps of Congress, this morning shortly before eleven o'clock. Like I said, nobody is sure what the statement is about, but there are rumors that it will involve a greater independence of Andalusia from Madrid..."

He paused and looked to where a black limousine was pulling up opposite the steps.

"I think this may be him now—"

As he spoke the doors opened and three men got out. Two were in dark suits and one was dressed in a blue blazer with an open shirt and chinos. He held a folder in his hand. The two suits closed in on him and he strode through the crowd toward the steps, one of them either side. He climbed seven of the thirteen steps, stopped and turned. Behind and above him, four cops with assault rifles emerged from the palace, fanned out and stood looking down at the crowd.

The camera crews closed in, swarming up the stairs to surround him, while a cluster of microphones bristled in front of him. Benjamin Musa gazed out at the crowd.

"Andalusia!" He almost yelled the word. "Andalusia, for five thousand years or more, Andalusia was the heart of the Iberian peninsula. From legendary Tartesos, the most powerful city on the Atlantic, to Cordoba, the second city of the Roman empire, Cordoba again as the Light of the West, the seat of the Caliphs, the most powerful city in Europe.

"But now we are the agricultural backwater of Spain, exploited by Madrid, by Catalonia, by the Basque Country, exploited by tourists and expatriates from all over Europe, exploited by Brussels. Today, we are a shadow of our former glory."

He nodded, looking at the journalists, at the cameras, one by one.

"Until now," he said. "Today, I bring news to the people of Spain, I bring news to the Congress, and I bring news *for* the people of Andalusia. Our servitude in Spain, and in the European Union is finished. Today, we rise again to our former glory. Today, the proud people of Andalusia rise up and say, 'Enough!'"

He held up the folder for all to see and raised his voice.

"I hold here a report. A report which I have commissioned in secret, because I know the nefarious forces which are at work in this building behind me. Forces that would suppress this report and bury it, to keep the Andalusian people under the Spanish yoke. But this report proves beyond any doubt that Andalusia rests on one of the biggest reserves of crude oil in the world. Andalusia is rich! And it is time we honored our heritage and took our place among the great, oil-rich nations of the Mediterranean. Listen to me, and listen carefully. This is not Spanish oil, this is not European oil, this is Andalusian oil. Spain, Brussels, you want our oil? *Os den por culo!* You can come and make a line and buy it!"

With that he turned and ran up the remaining six steps with his bodyguards at his side, and disappeared into the parliamentary building.

CHAPTER 2

THE PHONE WAS RINGING AND I COULD NOT breathe. I opened my eyes. Everything was pitch black and somebody was pushing a cushion down on my face. My lungs were screaming for air. The phone rang violently. I lurched and sat up, clawing at my face. Manny Pacquiao, my obnoxious cat, took a swipe at me and dropped off the bed.

I grabbed at the phone on my bedside table and spoke with difficulty.

"Yeah."

"Did you see it?"

I leaned back against the pillows and rolled my eyes.

"Sir, it's five in the morning. All I have seen is my cat's furry underbelly while he tried to suffocate me."

"Your facetiousness is inappropriate at the moment, Mason. Be in my office in half an hour. Don't shower. It takes too long."

I hung up and Manny Pacquiao leered at me from the top of the wardrobe as I made my way to the shower.

Thirty-five minutes later I was buzzed into Nero's office on Wilson Boulevard, in Rosslyn. He had what you could only describe as baleful eyes and he watched me with them as I sat down.

"Well?" he asked me.

"Well, what, sir?"

"Did you see it, confound it!"

"I told you, all I saw was my cat's belly. I was asleep. Most people are asleep at five AM, sir."

"Ridiculous." He pressed a button on his desk. A female voice said, "Yes, sir?"

"Coffee. Croissants. Is Lovelock there?"

"No sir, she's at home. This is Joyce."

"Good grief! Joyce?" He said it like he didn't believe anyone was really called Joyce. "Coffee, fresh butter croissants, fresh cream, butter. Lovelock knows..."

"Yes sir."

He released the button, looked at me and drew breath. I said, "I didn't see it, sir. I still don't know what 'it' is."

"You were not alerted by contacts in the press that an event was brewing in Spain this morning?"

"No, sir. Does this mean I don't get breakfast?" He stared at me until I realized I had asked the wrong question. "What happened in Madrid, sir?"

"Benjamin Musa, the leader of the socialist opposition in the Andalusian parliament, has called for Andalusian independence."

I looked at the window behind his head, where the horizon was turning a translucent gray-blue, and wondered whether the glass was bulletproof.

"I am not well up on Spanish politics, sir, but I seem to

remember Catalonia declared independence a few years back, the Basques had a long tradition of bombing their way to freedom, they had a civil war in '36 before which all the parliamentarians used to scream death threats at each other across the chamber."

"Your point?"

"I think it's the Mediterranean temperament. They are genetically predisposed to threaten to kill each other and declare independence. The Italians do it to."

The door opened and a nice lady in a blue cardigan came in with a large tray of croissants, coffee, butter and cream. She set it on the desk, smiled at us in order of relative importance and said, "There you are, dears. If you need anything, just shout."

When the door had closed he said, "Joyce," thoughtfully before pouring coffee.

"Spain is a prominent member of the European Union. It is composed of autonomous regions, each with its own parliament and executive, rather like a federation. Spain is potentially a rich country, but if the communities split apart, Spain's economy would collapse. Andalusia is a huge source of revenue, from tourism, shipping and not least, olive oil. If Andalusia seceded, Spain would become bankrupt."

I was stuffing a croissant into my mouth and held up two fingers.

"One, what's it to us, and two, surely the people of Andalusia would not be that stupid. They need Spain as much as Spain needs them."

"That was true, Alex, but it seems Benjamin Musa commissioned a secret report into deep-lying crude oil deposits beneath Andalusia. Spain's oil deposits have always been considered negligible, though its geology seemed promising. This report reveals, however, that the cavities that held the oil beneath the surface collapsed when the sierras were formed—quite recently in geological time—and the oil reserves drained down to a lower, more inaccessible level. This is important for two reasons."

He stuffed a croissant into his mouth and chewed, watching me. I knew this was my cue to sound intelligent.

"The technology," I said and he nodded. I went on. "The technology to produce this report didn't exist, so where did Musa get the technology?"

"To produce the report and extract the oil."

"OK, and..."

"The only people who have that technology, and it is truly cutting edge, are the Russians. While the West has been gearing up to phase out oil, Russia has been developing extraordinarily sophisticated equipment to find and exploit deep deposits."

"Oh." I nodded slowly as the implications began to dawn on me. "So the Russians have supplied the leader of the Andalusian socialist opposition with a plausible motive to declare independence and promise the people of Andalusia the kind of prosperity they can only dream of today,"

"While shouting about Madrid and Brussels stealing their wealth."

"This is revenge for Ukraine. They are putting a Russian puppet state—not on NATO's doorstep, right inside the door."

"We need to know how far Russia is prepared to go, how far Musa is prepared to go—"

"And perhaps more to the point," I interrupted, "how far Madrid is prepared to go."

"I was coming to that. Musa made his declaration just over an hour ago, and there is apparently a furious debate going on right now inside the parliamentary chamber in Congress. But there are some worrying features to this, Alex. The first is Musa's language. He has always made a thing of Andalusia's Mediterranean heritage, but lately, and today in particular, he has been stressing Andalusia's Arab past. Cordoba, in Southern Spain, was a powerful empire under the Ummayad caliphs. It sounds as though he is making overtures to his Arab and North African neighbors to form some kind of alliance."

"That brings Islam as well as oil into the mix."

"Precisely. The Arab nations have long considered Al-andalus—Andalusia to us—to be an Arab state, robbed from them by the Spanish. Now, if this posturing slides into civil unrest, or indeed civil war, and a foreign nation should lend Andalusia support, either overtly or covertly—remember, we are talking about some of the richest oil reserves on the planet, a prize worth risking war for..."

I finished for him. "Madrid could call on its NATO allies and we could see war in Europe for the first time in eighty years."

"So the question is, as you said, how far are the parties prepared to go? The prize is enormous. I fear they will be prepared to go all the way." He heaved a huge sigh that ended as a big grunt. "Twice since Vietnam, the CIA has lured Russia into wars that have all but crippled her economically. Afghanistan ultimately caused the collapse of the Soviet Union, along with a few other contributing factors.

This was a deliberate strategy by the Central Intelligence Agency. But now it seems someone in Moscow has very skillfully turned the tables on us, and unless we can pull something very clever out of our hat, I see us on a slippery slide, headed for a very costly, destructive war in Europe."

"What do you want me to do?"

"I don't know, but you had better be ready to travel to Spain at short notice. With a bit of luck all this posturing will resolve itself into the European Council and Madrid giving Andalusia—and Benjamin Musa—some kind of privileged position, and his backing off from the brink of war. We'll see what comes out of this meeting of the Congress today. The Spanish president is due to make a statement late this afternoon." The eyebrow he arched at me was as baleful as the dark eye beneath it. "You might try to watch it."

"I will." I nodded. "I will try to watch it."

I left and as I passed through the antechamber where Lovelock usually sat, I found Joyce in her blue cardigan. She was sewing a button onto a huge pair of pants. She smiled and I frowned.

"Are those...?"

"Mm-hmm."

"Does he know...?"

She shook her head and looked oddly satisfied. "I've been with him for years. He has no idea."

I rode the elevator down to the parking garage reflecting on the fact that it is often that which is most obviously in front of our noses that we are least aware of. Manny Pacquiao lying on my face, the Russians searching for oil in southern Spain, a woman in your house whose been stitching your pants for the last ten years and you don't know she's there. These are the things that can kill you, and you're just not aware of them.

I drove home in my TVR Griffith and started packing a suitcase. At eight I went down to the kitchen and made a proper breakfast of bacon, eggs, toast and sausages, along with a pint of espresso coffee, and sat watching the news while I ate.

They were already calling it the Spanish Crisis. Some guy on the BBC tried to coin "Spaxit," but I didn't think that was going to catch on. Besides sounding like a mental condition, it didn't cover the issue by a long shot. This wasn't just Spain following Britain back to independence from the Euro-Empire. This was Spain disintegrating like all the glue was melting.

After rehashing the basics, CNN cut to footage taken inside the Spanish Parliament, where Jesus Sanchez, the leader of the right wing Popular Party, and the president of the Spanish government, was making a statement. Over there it was apparently three PM lunchtime in the Med, and everyone would be glued to their TVs.

He was surprisingly young. He made his way to the lectern in a dark-blue suit with an open shirt. Obviously ties were not the big thing in Spain. I find it hard to vote for any politician, but a politician without a tie? That's like somebody saying to you, "I'm going to sit here for four years and get paid a lot of money for doing pretty much nothing—and I am not even going to *pretend* to be serious about my job."

I don't know if Jesius Sanchez was serious or if he was putting on a show, but whatever it was, it was convincing. His face was taut and there was real anger in his eyes. As he started talking the voice of a simultaneous interpreter kicked in over the top on the TV.

"We have heard a lot in recent months, weeks and days, about the glorious heritage of Andalusia, the Caliphs of Cordoba, the eight hundred years during which Andalusia was not occupied by the Arabs, but during which Al-andalus was a shining light of Arab culture in Europe. Eight-hundred-years."

He leaned on the dispatch box, nodding, looking around at the congressmen and women. Then he leaned forward and spoke like he was fighting to control his anger.

"Fourteen hundred and ninety-two! Over five hundred and thirty years ago, the last Arabs were expelled from Granada! I would like to ask Mr. Musa, how many years does Andalusia have to be integrated within Spain before it becomes Spanish! A thousand years? Two thousand years?"

He paused, looking around again. He was not reading from notes. This was spontaneous and he meant it.

"I would say to Mr. Musa, and to *all* Spaniards, that integration does not come from years of domination, but from integration. And I will tell this house and this nation *right now* that no part of Spain is more intimately identified with Spanish culture and Spanish identity than Andalusia. What could be more Spanish than flamenco, the Giralda of Seville, the cathedral of Cordoba or the Alhambra of Granada? Andalusia is at the heart of the Spanish soul, and to deny that Andalusia is Spanish is to deny that Spain exists at all!"

Another pause and he actually wiped tears from his eyes.

"So why? Why is Mr. Musa engaging in this attempt against the integrity of the kingdom? Why, when Spain is finally prospering in democratic union with the wider Europe, when we are finally emerging from the economic crises that have hurt us so badly as a nation, why does he now seek to destroy our homeland and our kingdom?" He nodded. "I will tell you."

He poured water from a decanter and sipped.

"I will tell you: because he is hungry for the power that he thinks will come to him from an independent, oil-rich Andalusia, because he is blinded by his own greed, because he does not see the economic crisis that he will precipitate and the poverty and hardship he will bring down upon his own people, because he is *blind* to the inevitable imposition of Islam on Andalusia as a precondition to his joining this famous 'Mediterranean Club' of oil-rich countries. But above all, ladies, gentlemen, people of Spain, because he does not *care*, just so long as he can exercise personal control over that oil."

He paused again and stood, leaning on the dispatch box, staring down at the space between his hands. When he looked up, his face was tight, pale, drawn with anger.

"But if I give you the impression that I am asking Mr. Musa to desist and withdraw his demand for independence, then forgive me. Because I have not expressed myself correctly. Let me be clear. The oil beneath Andalusia does not belong to Andalusia any more than the fish from Galicia belongs to Galicia or the steel from the Basque Country belongs to the Basques. That oil belongs to the Spanish people, and if—*if*—a decision is taken *by the Spanish government* to exploit that oil, then it will be done for the benefit of Spain.

"And let me make a final couple of points: there will be

no referendum on the independence of Andalusia, there will be no parliamentary debate on the subject, and if Mr. Musa persists in his attempts to destroy the union of the Kingdom, he faces trial for treason. We, in this house, must be tireless in protecting the integrity of Spain, and the benefit of *all* the Spanish people. *Viva España!*"

There was a lot of applause. My own feeling was that he'd done a good job, and I could imagine that all eyes in the European Commission and the European Council must have been glued on him. Right now it was a storm in a teacup. But if Musa was the right—or more accurately, the *wrong* kind of man, this could turn into a major constitutional crisis, or worse. After all, as Nero had said, we were not dealing with carrots, or even wheat, we were dealing with some of the largest oil reserves on the planet, at a time when oil was running out and there was still no credible alternative.

CHAPTER 3

Jesus Sanchez was in the back of his dark blue Audi S8, watching the lights of Madrid slip by in the night. Beside him was Alvaro Romero, the man who had been his ally and friend for the last fifteen years. Romero watched the president—the president he had created—and saw the anxiety ill concealed on his face.

"This will blow over," he told him. "Just as Tejero's coup blew over, just as Catalan independence blew over. Social progress is a relentless force, Jesus. It is like gravity, it draws us ever closer to the center. First it was Rome, then it was the Vatican, then it was London, Washington DC, now it is Brussels."

Jesus flicked his eyes at him. "Philosophy, Alvaro. This is not a time for philosophy. This is a pragmatic problem."

"That's what I am trying to tell you." He paused, watched the light and shadow from the streetlamps wash over his friend's face. "You must been seen to be reacting energetically, appeal to the people, enlist the support of the king, but be confident. Benjamin has no hope of success. This play of his is childish."

They pulled onto the Gran Via and moved toward the Carretera de la Princesa. The leaves of the plane trees mottled the light from the streetlamps. Sanchez watched the subway stations slip by. The shops were open still. They wouldn't close till nine or nine thirty, and people swarmed on the sidewalks, lightly dressed for the heat.

Jesus turned to study his friend's face. "Putin's invasion of Chechnya was childish, but childish men hungry for power do childish, reckless things. I have known Benjamin for many years. He tried to blackmail me—"

"I remember. I told him if he persisted I would have some people break both his legs."

Jesus's eyebrows rose high on his brow. "You did that?"

Alvaro laughed. "Of course not. How could the future deputy president of Spain do such a thing. I got somebody else to do it for me."

They both laughed. But the laughter soon died and Jesus's eyes were drawn to the vast edifice of the headquarters of the air force: the Army of the Air, they called it. They slipped past and onto the circus around the Arco de la Victoria of the Moncloa, brightly lit in the night. Sanchez pointed at it.

"Built by Franco to commemorate his victory against the Republicans. That civil war lasted three years, Alvaro, and was triggered by small, greedy men and women driven by ideology, who threatened murder and war, screaming across the floor at each other in Congress. Today reminded me of that. We cannot have that again."

Alvaro slapped him on the shoulder as the great stone arch swept by.

"Come on, Jesus! They were other times. The whole of Europe was destabilized, Germany's power was growing, Italy was torn between fascists and communists, the Balkans were unstable and everybody was terrified of what Russia might do next—"

Sanchez interrupted, half laughing. "Is this supposed to calm me? Are you talking about 1936 or 2023?" He wagged a finger at his friend. "And don't forget a very important dynamic, Alvaro, which we have today which was missing in '36. The stability of the past seventy years has not been thanks to the monolith of the European Union, it has been due to the steady flow of abundant energy to drive our industrial, commercial and social machinery. That energy is coming to an end, and we still have no credible alternative to replace it. And suddenly we find that Andalusia holds reserves that could keep us going for another century. That kind of power, Alvaro, can drive a man like Putin, or a man like Benjamin, to do crazy things."

They had left the Arco de la Victoria behind them and were now speeding among leafy suburbs toward the Palacio de la Moncloa, the president's official residence in Madrid. Alvaro was nodding.

"You're right," he said simply as they approached the Plaza Cardenal Cisneros underpass. Alvaro looked out the window to his left as a large SUV with tinted windows drew alongside. The front passenger window opened and a man in a balaclava leaned out with a pump action shotgun. He fired twice and their driver's head exploded in a shower of blood, gore and glass.

Jesus swore and screamed out his friend's name. Next thing the SUV rammed the Audi and drove it against the wall of the tunnel, spitting a shower of sparks up the grimy wall until the car came to a halt. Alvaro kicked open the rear door, smashing it against the rear of the van. He was screaming like a maniac. Jesus saw him grappling with a gunman. It was a second only, then the gunman was beating him to the ground. A fraction of a second later another man in a balaclava leaned in holding an assault rifle. Jesus said, "No," and the man emptied the magazine into the president of the government.

There were thirty-six rounds in the magazine. There was very little left of the president.

There were three men. They were wearing latex gloves, overalls and balaclavas. While two of them stripped off their masks and overalls, the third pulled a Glock 17 and put two rounds into Alvaro where he lay beside the car. He then stripped off his overalls and his mask too. All three men were completely bald.

There was chaos in the tunnel. Several cars had collided behind them and most of the traffic was trying to reverse away from the shooting. An Audi A4 pulled up. The three men climbed in and accelerated away to lose themselves in the spaghetti junction at Manzanares, just one mile away.

It was almost half an hour before the police cars, Guardia Civil antiterrorist squad and scene of crime forensic teams were able to get to the scene and cordon it off. Before that a helicopter ambulance flew in and found a badly beaten, injured Alvaro Romero on the road, and what was left of Jesus Sanchez, the president, in the back of his limousine.

When it was reported on the news the nation went into shock.

At twelve midnight a special, emergency session of parliament was called, and as Alvaro Romero entered the chamber, with his right arm in a sling and his face swollen and disfigured, purple and blue from the beating he had received, there was a collective gasp from all sides of the chamber. A doctor and a nurse attended him, but he walked, steady and unwavering, to the dispatch box. He didn't falter.

"Today, Spain has lost a great leader, a man who was an idealist and a pragmatist, a creative visionary, and a sound administrator, a politician who was also an incorruptible human being. Spain has lost all this, but I have lost more."

His tortured face twisted, his bottom lip curled in and he made no effort to hide his sobs. "I have lost all that, and also a brother and a friend. But I stand before you, the nation, here today and I tell you that the injuries I carry on my body are nothing compared to the injuries I bear in my heart and my soul! I am here to tell you that, as deputy president of the government I, here and now, step into the shoes of Jesus Sanchez, and if I stand here, talking to you, it is as though he were here himself!

"Whoever did this, I *swear* to you that they will not derail our dream and our project. I am ordering now, as of this very instant, the most thorough investigation into this brutal, savage murder. The investigation will be conducted by General Diego Carmona Sanchez, supreme commander of the Guardia Civil, and I swear to you on the blood of my fallen brother, that his death will be avenged and the enemies of Spain will be hunted down like rabid dogs and *exterminated!*"

There was heavy silence that spoke as much of shock as of awe before the extraordinary events that had risen before them. A moment later Alvaro Romero faltered and his doctor and his nurses rushed forward to support him. Seconds after that a gurney was rushed into the chamber and the acting president of the government was wheeled away.

The next day the press and the television news were completely dominated by, on the one hand the word "Exterminated," which appeared on just about every headline in Europe, and the question being asked by every congressman in Madrid, was the deputy president in a fit condition to step into the late president's shoes, or should they call a new general election. Benjamin Musa was among those vociferously calling for a general election. It would serve, he said, as a referendum to decide whether the people of Andalusia wanted to secede from Spain. But just about every right wing and moderate journalist and politician agreed that this was a time when Spain needed certainty and clarity, and a capable pair of hands. The dilemma was, was Alvaro Romero that pair of hands, or was he too emotionally and physically scarred to take charge of a powder keg as volatile as this one?

But, by that evening Alvaro Romero once again astonished the nation by appearing once again in public, this time on the steps of the Gregorio Marañon University Hospital, still with his arm in a sling and a badly battered face, but with a different demeanor and a different look in his eyes. He waved away the questions from reporters.

"I am going to make a simple statement. I am on my way now to the Moncloa to start work where Jesus Sanchez, the president, left off. Our program and our project for this country will continue unchanged. I will be briefed tonight on the progress of the investigation into Jesus's murder, and if I find there are adequate grounds, and that this was an act of terrorism by those wishing to tear this country apart, then I will declare a state of emergency. That is all I have to say for today."

His security team crowded around him and he was bundled down to his waiting car, and driven away into the growing dusk.

Maybe, as his car's red tail lights receded into the gathering gloom, he was thinking that his veiled threat would be enough to make Benjamin Musa back off. Maybe. Or perhaps he knew better than that.

In fact Benjamin Musa, already back in his corner office in Seville, had been working feverishly all day, calling in favors, applying thumbscrews and offering powerful inducements and bribes. He knew that this was his one shot. He would probably never get another. So he had to hit the bull right in the eye.

By the time Alvaro Romero climbed, exhausted into the back of his Audi, and took off for the palace of the Moncloa, Benjamin Musa was stretching out his legs and sipping a large Macallan whisky. He had secured an extraordinary, plenary session of the Andalusian Parliament for nine AM the next morning. He would make his case for independence, put forward a secondary motion for a referendum on independence, put both motions to the vote, and he knew— he knew because he had tied up every god damned loose end —he knew the motion for independence would be carried by a landslide majority.

He smiled, and then laughed. What a mess, he told himself. What an almighty mess he had created! He threw back his head and laughed out loud. What an almighty, holy mess!

Scan the QR code below to purchase FLASHPOINT.
Or go to: righthouse.com/flashpoint

NOTES

CHAPTER 15

1. See Alex Mason 3, *Mason's Law*

.

www.ingramcontent.com/pod-product-compliance
Lightning Source LLC
Chambersburg PA
CBHW031123210626
46816CB00016B/2070